Published by Pine Veil Press
www.pineveilpress.com

Print ISBN: 978-1-971147-03-1
EBook ISBN: 978-1-971147-02-4

First Edition

Printed in the United States of America

For information, inquiries, or permissions, please contact the publisher or author.

Table of Contents

Author's Note

This novel falls within the realm of Dark Drama and Fantasy, yet its foundation is deeply human. Each story explores death—the reaping of souls after their earthly journey ends, however that end may come.

As a mortician with three decades of experience, I have walked alongside grief in its rawest forms. My work has always been about care—both for the departed and for those left behind. That same reverence carries through these pages.

If you are currently mourning a loved one, I encourage you to pause until you feel ready to read on. Some stories confront suicide and other difficult themes. If you or someone you know is struggling, please reach out for help. There is always someone who cares, and help is always within reach.

Many of these stories draw from real encounters with life and death—truths reshaped through fiction. Names and details have been altered for privacy and, admittedly, a touch of self-preservation.

Read, reflect, and debate. I look forward to the conversations that follow.

Life once asked Death, "Why do people love me and hate you?"

And Death replied, "Because you are a beautiful lie, and I am the ugly truth"

Chapter 1: Why Me?

Does a life story begin with a first breath—or the last? Maybe it depends on who's asking.

For Drake Themus, it begins on a cool evening in Armendariz Cemetery.

Twilight drapes the marble rows. On a granite bench, a lone man hunches forward, his face streaked with dried tears. Drake lifts his head; pain and fury war behind his eyes. Across from him, his wife's name glimmers in the moonlight—twenty years of marriage carved into stone by a drunk driver's reckless behavior.

He exhales, a sound halfway between a sigh and a sob and the empty bottle of Johnny Walker Blue whiskey slips from his hands.

A breeze slides over his skin, sharp as glass. He shudders, straightens, and peers into the dark. A figure gathers there, a ripple in the night, coalescing into a dark, foreboding form.

Every sense sparks at once. He knows that silhouette from every story ever whispered: the Grim Reaper, Thanatos, Azrael, Angel of Death—take your pick.

Drake rises, legs unsteady, voice rough. "Are you here for me?"

The hooded shape answers in a voice that seems to come from the earth itself."Yes. But I'm not here to take your soul. I'm here to speak about your afterlife."

"My afterlife?" Drake lets out a dry laugh. "I'm pretty sure one has to be dead for that. Thirty years as a mortician have at least taught me that much."

"Precisely. That's why I'm interested in you and your afterlife. Thirty years is a long time to walk among the dead."

Drake blinks, the exchange twisting his thoughts. "I've handled death's leftovers," he says, "even pronounced it a few times—but I've only had one firsthand experience." He glances at the mausoleum. His throat tightens, but no tears come.

"There are, on average, sixty-two million deaths each year," the Grim Reaper continues. "Two every second of every minute of every day. Forever. I know this because I am the Lord of Death. You may call me Lord Grim. Every soul is my responsibility."

Drake's head spins. *I must have drunk more than usual.*

Lord Grim tilts his hood slightly. "Yes, Drake, you're drunk—but not that drunk. And no, I'm not a hallucination. I am the Grim Reaper, and as I said, I'm here about your afterlife. Shall I continue?"

Drake exhales the single word. "Yes."

"Good." Lord Grim's tone softens. "I have many who serve beneath me—Disease, Murder, Accident, to name a few. Each carries different gifts. One position has been vacant for some time, and I believe you are suited to it."

Drake squints up at the hood. "So you're offering me a job? A promotion? As what—another Reaper? Come on. Where's the camera? This is a setup." He laughs once, scanning the shadows for proof of the prank.

"This is no joke. You have a choice: become the Reaper of Justice… or you—"

Drake cuts in. "How can I choose when I don't even know what a Reaper does, let alone a Reaper of Justice?"

Lord Grim exhales, a sound like wind through dry leaves. "Drake, you are a smart man."

Silence stretches. Drake inhales the night, grief and disbelief wrestling for ground. The Reaper lifts one skeletal arm and points toward the mausoleum.

Drake turns. A dark figure lies motionless at the base of the marble. The truth hits him like a hammer. The chill that swept through him earlier hadn't been Death's arrival—it had been the instant his own life ended.

A thin mist begins to creep through Armendariz Cemetery, coiling around headstones and drifting across the marble path. The full moon hangs low, pouring silver light over the graves.

From somewhere in the distance comes a single caw, low and hollow. Then—the whisper of wings. Talons click softly against granite.

A raven lands on the bench beside Drake's still body and begins to pace, its feathers catching the moonlight like oil on water. The sound seems to pull at him, tugging his awareness forward until his mind forms one word that echoes through the hollow of his chest: *void*.

Void—because everything human within him has vanished. Fear. Regret. Desire. Even time.

Time, he realizes, has no meaning here.

He stands motionless, staring at the raven, and the thought comes unbidden: *I have a choice. Become a Reaper, carve out a future in death—or face my eternal judgment.*

He turns toward the hooded figure. His throat feels dry as dust when he forces out the words.

"I'll do it. I'll be a Reaper for you."

"Excellent," Lord Grim replies, the voice echoing like stone grinding in a tomb. He begins to withdraw into the fog.

"Wait—" Drake calls out. "That's it? I have questions."

Lord Grim halts, black robe billowing in the night air. "Ask."

Drake shifts his weight, uneasy beneath the gaze of the unseen face. "You said I'd be the *Reaper of Justice*. What does that mean?"

"It means," Lord Grim says, stepping closer, "you will collect the souls who must die for the betterment of humankind."

"The *betterment* of humankind?" Drake frowns. "I don't understand what that means."

"There are those whose choices disrupt the balance," Lord Grim replies, his tone dropping to something almost gentle. "Balance must always be kept or restored. I decide who and when. As the Reaper of Justice, you will carry out that purpose."

Drake stands silent, the weight of it pressing into him.

"That is all you need to know for now."

With that, Lord Grim dissolves into mist, leaving only the whisper of wings and the faint shimmer of moonlight on marble. Drake turns in a slow circle, searching the darkness, but the night is empty.

Only the raven remains, its eyes gleaming like twin coals—watching, waiting.

Chapter 2: Chamber of Entrance

Drake becomes aware—aware of himself, of a body that isn't quite a body, of space. The fog from the cemetery dissolves, and he finds he is seated at a long, dark table in a vast chamber. His chair sits on the right side, midway down. Across the expanse, at the point of the great V-shaped table, rises a throne carved from obsidian and bone. A massive scythe rests against its side, the blade curving like a crescent of frozen moonlight.

Lord Grim sits upon that throne, hood shadowing whatever face he might have. His voice rolls through the chamber like distant thunder.

"Welcome, Drake. This is the Chamber of Entrance. It lies between the earthly realm and the great beyond. All souls we reap pass through here to be judged for the choices they made and the truths they believed."

His tone deepens, almost ceremonial.

"You exist in two places now: the earth you left behind, and this chamber—our meeting place, our crossroads. As the Reaper of Justice, most of your work will occur in the earthly realm, among the living. But here is where the reapers gather, learn, and answer to me."

A sudden flutter of wings snaps through the stillness. A raven streaks across the chamber, its black feathers slicing the air. It slips through a towering archway at the far end, and as soon as the iron doors behind it close, the locks slam home with a metallic clang that echoes through the chamber.

Lord Grim's head tilts slightly, as if acknowledging the interruption.

"You will notice the birds," he says. "They are not adornment."

The chamber seems to listen.

"Those who sit to my right—Justice among them —are bound to ravens. Ravens are witnesses. They observe, remember, and return. They serve reapers whose work demands discernment, restraint, and consequence weighed against truth."

The air shifts, colder.

"To my left sit reapers whose charge is chaos made inevitable—War, Accident, Disease, Murder. Their companions are crows. Crows are harbingers. They do not linger. They announce what must happen and move on."

Lord Grim's presence presses down, final and immovable.

He gestures toward the expanse of the table. "Each Reaper has a place here. These places must be respected."

Then he vanishes—no sound, no mist, just absence.

For a moment, Drake sits unmoving. "What have I done?" he murmurs.

Eventually he rises, exploring the rest of the chamber. It is cathedral-like in size, but colder, older. The archway where the raven disappeared stands two stories high. Its twin iron doors glow from within—white light on the right, fiery red on the left. Drake shivers.

Heaven or hell, he thinks. Or whatever versions exist for souls who cross this place.

He turns back to the table, noting the twelve chairs flanking the throne—six on each side. Names shimmer faintly above them in symbols he somehow understands.

To the right of Lord Grim sit the seats of Elder, Lullaby, Seppuku, Vengeance, Exonerate... and Justice. His seat.

To the left: War, Accident, Disease, Fear, Murder... and one whose name is deliberately erased. Only a smooth strip of dark metal marks the place where a title once existed.

Drake lingers on that empty space. A chill slides through him.

16

Behind the chairs, alcoves are carved into the walls. Each contains a perch of blackened iron—some long and curved, others jagged and forked.

As he steps into the open center of the V-shape, a raven materializes on one of the perches. Its feathers glint like wet obsidian. It tilts its head toward Drake before it launches into flight.

Lord Grim appears once again upon the throne, his presence filling the chamber.

"All ravens are named," he says. "This one is Conroy—Conroy belongs to Elder."

The bird swoops low, then disappears into shadow.

"For now, Drake, you will remain here. I will summon you soon."

The throne empties once more, leaving Drake alone with the silent table and the distant echo of wings.

The silence stretches, and without meaning to, his thoughts drift to Alyssa again—the weight of her body curled against him as she sobbed out her grief, the hollow stare at her mother's funeral. Is she crying tonight? Will she believe he's simply… gone? Or worse—will she think he chose to leave her?

Chapter 3: Elder

Sunlight glints across the gilded letters of a sign: Graceful Living Retirement Facility.

Birds sing. Cars drift past. A dog barks somewhere down the block, and a faint siren wails in the distance. The living call places like this 'Heaven's waiting room'— a fitting description as Lord Grim and the newest Reaper of Justice materialize across the street from the entrance.

The two stand in silence for a long moment. Justice takes in every detail. Nothing appears unusual, yet everything feels extraordinary—the warmth of the sun on his skin, the sharp green scent of cut grass, the clear trill of the birds. Death has heightened his senses.

He blinks, and Lord Grim is already halfway to the door.

"Not paying attention on my first day," Justice mutters. "Perfect."

He steps into the street and instantly jerks back as cars speed past. Dazed for a moment, he watches them blur by—horns blaring, the rush of air tugging at his coat —and then it clicks— earthly rules don't apply to him anymore. He ditches the "look both ways before crossing" rule, and steps off the curb once more with confidence.

"First encounters with the living world can be tricky," Lord Grim says, his voice even and low.

"Yeah, I guess the first step's a doozy," Justice quips playfully.

Grim does not smile. "You'll begin reaping soon. For now, you'll shadow another. This is Elder—the most experienced and the wisest of the Reapers. Listen carefully and feel free to ask questions."

"Thank you, Lord Grim," says a woman with deep olive skin and dark eyes as she steps forward. Her hair, pure white, is wrapped in a woven scarf that frames an ageless face. Tranquility radiates from her.

"Justice," she says warmly, "welcome. As Lord Grim stated, I am the Reaper named Elder, and yes—I've held this position the longest. Let's proceed."

Before Justice can answer, she glides through the doors of Graceful Living.

The lobby overwhelms him. Walkers squeak, wheelchairs rattle, aides call instructions over the hum of conversation. The air smells faintly of disinfectant and overbrewed coffee.

Frozen, Justice turns from side to side, trying to take it all in.

Elder doubles back, her tone that of a patient teacher. "Oh, sweet new one. They can't see us. Move with confidence. Remember your purpose."

He exhales, centers himself, and follows. This time he passes through the hall effortlessly, unnoticed by the living.

At the middle of the corridor Elder stops before a door marked Bethany W. and Simona C.

"This is us," she says. "Are you ready?"

"I'm as ready as I'll ever be."

The room is bright, and the far wall is filled with windows overlooking a garden of fruiting trees and blooming flowers. One bed is neatly made, a worn teddy bear resting on its pillow and framed photographs lined along a low shelf—children, grandchildren, crayon drawings faded with time. Beside it, an elderly woman sits in a recliner, quietly murmuring a string of names in prayer, and begging for death to take her.

The second bed lies closest to the door. A handmade quilt is draped over an ashen figure.

Justice's voice drops. "Why does she look... void of color?"

"That's how we know," Elder answers gently. "The body empties when the soul is ready to leave."

She steps forward, lowering her voice. "Bethany, I am here. Your earthly pain is over. It is time."

A shadow crosses the window. A raven lands on the sill, raps once against the glass, then takes flight.

Justice doesn't look away from the bed. "Why isn't anyone rushing in?" he asks. "There are no machines. No alarms. No one calling for help." His brow furrows. "Why is no one trying to save her?"

Simona's voice rises behind them, trembling. "Dear Lord Jesus, hear my plea. I am tired and not afraid. I am ready to go home."

Justice turns sharply, caught by the contrast. "She's begging to die," he says, gesturing toward Simona, "and yet she's still here." His gaze returns to Bethany. "Yet Bethany, she's—she's gone."

Elder follows his gaze. "Because they have tried."

Justice's jaw tightens. "How hard?"

"Every way mortals know," Elder replies. "Doctors. Medicines. Procedures. Waiting. Hoping. There comes a moment when saving a body only prolongs suffering."

Justice shakes his head. "So they stop?"

21

"They release," Elder says. "There is a difference."

Justice exhales slowly, then gestures again toward the recliner. "And her? She's praying for death."

Elder turns toward Simona, her expression tender. "Simona is faithful—but she is not ready. She has lived a long, full life. Five children. Two husbands. Decades of love, grief, joy, and loss. Wanting to go is not the same as being prepared to go."

She pauses. "Her prayers will be answered when her purpose here is complete."

Justice stands between the two beds now, visibly torn. One soul pleading for release. One abandoned by exhaustion and acceptance.

"So one stays because her life still holds meaning," he says quietly. "And one leaves because the world has decided it no longer does."

Elder meets his eyes. "No. One leaves because her soul has finished what it came to do."

Justice looks back at Bethany, unease settling deep in his chest.

Elder's voice softens. "Don't worry — that feeling will leave you soon."

"What feeling?"

"The feeling that everyone must be saved," Elder replies.

Justice exhales slowly, torn between duty and doubt, and understands that death neither asks for—nor waits—for consent.

They step into the hall. The air ripples; the world blurs and reforms under harsh fluorescent light.

Justice blinks as a nurse hurries past—her form flickering from full color to gray and back again. The floor tilts beneath him.

"Justice!" Elder's voice cuts through the haze. He's on his knees before he knows he's fallen.

"I saw something," he gasps. "The nurse—she turned gray, and then I saw hands pressing a syringe into an IV port."

Elder kneels beside him, curious. "I am a little surprised you experienced it this early, Justice. This is foresight. The Reaper of Justice is the only one of the Reapers that can glimpse what's to come. You saw a death that hasn't yet happened."

He lets out a shaky laugh. "Lucky me."

"Not luck," she corrects softly. "Responsibility."

The light shifts again. They stand in a bustling corridor.

"Traveling gets easier," Elder says, touching his arm. "Welcome to Los Angeles General—one of the busiest hospitals in the world. Stay close; this place is a labyrinth."

They pause outside Room 7 in the ICU wing. Through the glass, a family surrounds a hospital bed, their heads bowed in prayer. Machines hum, lines wave and spike and then finally flatten into silence. A nurse notes the time.

Justice asks, "Elder, how is it with religious believers who pass?"

Elder responds with a smile, "Second Corinthians 5:8—'Absent from the body, present with the Lord.'"

A raven caws somewhere beyond the walls. The soul is gone.

"I keep hearing a bird caw," Justice peers toward the sound. "So the ravens and crows carry them?"

"They bear what we cannot," Elder replies. "We release the soul from the body; they deliver it. The final destination of the soul is not for us to know."

Her head tilts. "Another Reaper has entered the building. Come."

They turn down a brighter corridor crowded with relatives clutching balloons and flowers. Behind a wide expanse of glass, rows of bassinets fill a large sterile room.

"Life begins here," Elder says, "but not all of these new lives continue."

Inside, a pale red-haired girl in a yellow sundress moves between the cribs. She pauses, lifts a colorless infant, and cradles it close. A single tear slides down her cheek as her raven caws.

Justice swallows hard. "Who is she?"

"She is Lullaby," Elder whispers. "She tends to the smallest souls. Some are here only for a moment."

A memory flickers—Alyssa's small, precious body nestled against his chest just after she was born. No parent should outlive that touch.

"Come," Elder says gently, pulling him away. "One more lesson."

Justice is struck by how calming her touch is.

The ER bursts around them—monitors beeping, voices calling orders. Paramedics wheel in a woman bruised and trembling. "Thirty-year-old female," one reports. "Multiple contusions, possible facial fractures."

A commotion erupts in the lobby. A man storms in, shouting, "Where is my wife? I want to see my wife!" Security intercepts him. Justice's gaze locks on him—the man's skin is entirely gray.

A cold pulse grips him. The scene dissolves into darkness: a garage, a shovel, the smell of dirt, fear, and something far more sinister. A flashlight cuts a narrow beam across the concrete.

He blinks and the hospital returns.

Elder studies him. "Another foresight?"

"Yeah," he breathes. "That man—he will kill."

Her face is solemn. "And when he does, Lord Grim will send you."

The chaos of the ER fades into silence.

Elder places a hand on his arm. "Enough for today. You've learned well."

Justice hesitates. "May I ask—what was your name in life… and how many souls are you responsible for?"

A faint smile curves her lips. "Aryn," she says. "As for the rest—more than one lifetime could hold."

The world softens into white. Only the sound of wings remains—and the echo of a name that feels like grace.

Chapter 4: War

Finding himself back in the chamber, Justice sits with his head bowed, the weight of everything he has witnessed, pressing into him like a boulder. He closes his eyes, forcing each image—each soul—through his mind's eye, searching for meaning in the chaos.

A crack splits the air—loud and electric. Justice's head snaps toward the sound.

A massive figure fills the doorway: seven and a half feet of muscle and shadow, a mace leveled straight at him.

"WE ARE OFF!"

Justice blinks, startled, "Off where and who are you?"

The giant's eyes gleam with mischief, "Is it not obvious who I am, new one!?" He booms, raising his mace and striking a theatrical pose.

Justice, not clear if this question is rhetorical, answers, "Ares the God of War?"

The figure laughs, and the sound shakes the chamber. "No, of course not! There is only one God who created all and judges all. I am the Reaper of War! A humble General, from one of Earth's first battles.

Enough chit-chat. We are off to a massacre. I could use some help, so the souls of battle do not stay in limbo too long before their transport. Call your raven so we can be on our way."

"My raven? I don't have a…" a loud caw cuts him off. Justice slowly turns. A large raven perches on the beam behind his chair, his eyes as shiny as onyx.

War walks over to Justice, laughs and slaps him on the back. "I assume introductions are in order. Raven, this is Justice, and Justice, this is your raven. They serve better if given a name. What shall it be?"

Justice stares at the large black bird. Thinking to himself, *This is crazy, I have never named a bird in my life. How am I to just come up with a name?* That question brought back the memory of his wife and him deciding names for their first child: Alyssa for a girl and Devon for a boy. Just like that Justice says, "I will call him Devon."

"WELL DONE! That is a good strong English name meaning "Defender." With that taken care of it's time for us to go," and with that War and Justice, along with their birds, head off to the massacre.

Justice slowly opens and closes his eyes. A grassy valley comes into focus, yet it seems so far away. Justice realizes he is standing on the edge of a rocky cliff. The air is dry as parchment, but it carries a sweetness that has turned heavy with rot. Justice backs away to ward off the bile rising in his throat.

War lets out a roar of laughter. "Never smelled nerve gas before?"

"Where did that come from?"

"At dawn, Somali civil fighters were ambushed by jihadist militants," War says, scanning the haze. "They used gas to gain the upper hand—then bullets. These are the fallen: some are already gone, while some are trapped between dying and death."

Justice, still adjusting to his heightened perception of the living world, realizes he can hear the buzz of the flies as if they are in his ear along with the heady smell of gun smoke, thick in his lungs. Though all of this is miles away, Justice can still hear the voices of the men crying for mercy.

He turns to War, "Can we help them?"

With a stern gaze War replies, "No. They chose this path. Death was always their final commander. Our duty is to gather, not to save."

They descend into the carnage. The ground squelches underfoot. War moves with brutal efficiency, his crow swooping and returning in a steady rhythm. Justice mimics him, the motions mechanical at first—

reach, summon, release. But the cries won't stop. Some men still cling to life, their eyes wide and pleading.

"How do I understand them?" Justice asks, his voice tight. "I hear them speaking English—yet I know they are not."

War's laugh rumbles. "You think *I* speak your tongue? The only language I know died with Sodom and Gomorrah. Understanding is a gift. The Lord Grim allows us to hear what each soul needs, not necessarily what has been said."

Justice nods slowly with understanding. "Like the Tower of Babel—many tongues, one truth."

They continue the grim harvest. As Devon circles above, something flashes on a distant ridge. Justice squints and sees a man lowering binoculars, shouting orders to a group beside him. The men scatter, but the leader lingers—and fades, color draining from him like sand through glass.

Justice remembers Elder's warning and tucks the image away. "Who is that?" he asks.

War follows his gaze, his jaw tightening.

"That is General Khadir al-Bashir, the one who led this slaughter. A warlord by name, but a coward at heart. It will be one fine day when Justice comes for him. But for now, our work here is done."

They're back in the chamber before Justice can blink. War leans back, studying him.

"More questions?" he says with a grin.

Justice's gaze drifts to War's crow. "You said we can understand all languages. How do we *appear* to those who see us?"

War's grin fades into something thoughtful. "Not everyone can. The living rarely do. But to the dead—we look as they need us to. The faithful see angels. The grieving see family. The fearful... see mercy in whatever form they can bear."

Justice hesitates. "Could a Reaper appear as Jesus of Nazareth?"

A shadow crosses War's eyes. "Only once. That Reaper's face was stripped away and never seen again. No one imitates the Son of God and survives it. Anything else, your little mind is curious about?"

Justice smiles faintly. "When you walked the earth, what was your name?"

War's grin returns, broad and wild. "Bymascus Ideaous Liamos of Lilaea."

Justice chuckles. "That's a mouthful. Mind if I call you Bill?"

War throws his head back in laughter. "Bill! I like it. And you?"

"Drake Themus."

"Strong name, Drake." War stands, his crow shifting on his shoulder. "We'll be friends, you and I. For now, rest. You've earned it."

He vanishes in a shimmer of light.

Justice sinks into his chair. The silence feels heavier than battle. Exhaustion pulls at him, and he lets his eyes close—just for a moment

Chapter 5: Suicide

A faint breeze moves through the chamber. Justice stirs, his head still bowed, eyes closed. The whisper of wings echoes above him—slow, steady, rhythmic. One word flickers through his mind: *time.*

Drifting between waking and sleep, the word begins to multiply, circling him. *What is time? How do you measure it? Why does it exist?*

The questions blur into a single truth: *Time is a weapon. Time is a curse and a mercy. Time is a cage built inside the mind.*

His body shifts in the chair as the past begins to unfold. He sees himself—young, laughing, alive. The vision glows gold, and he thinks of it as *the golden age,* when time was something adults kept, not something that kept him.

The images race faster. The gold fades to gray. His eyes snap open.

There is no time anymore, he realizes—only memory. Time never really existed and never will again.

He rubs his face, trying to shake the thought and slowly looks to his left. Trying not to jump out of his chair, he sees another reaper a few chairs down from him —still, silent, and watching. The figure appears young, with an otherworldly calm and features that might have been Asian in life, though Justice can't be sure.

Without warning, the man stands and points directly at him.

Then the chamber dissolves.

He blinks into a new scene, disoriented.

A girl stands at a bathroom sink—maybe fourteen or fifteen. Her reflection trembles in the mirror; tears streak down her face. The air hums with dread.

"There's so much blood," Justice whispers.

"Hai," says the Reaper beside him—the only word he offers at first.

"Can we save her?" Justice asks.

"There is no saving hopelessness," the Reaper replies softly. "Despair has deep roots."

"Then why bring me here?"

"I bring you to understand." The young Reaper turns slightly toward him, eyes filled with quiet sorrow. "I am Seppuku, the Reaper—"

"I know seppuku," Justice cuts in. "Samurai history. Ritual death. Honor through the blade. You're the Reaper of Suicide.

"But she's just a child," he says, voice low.

"All who break beneath their pain are children," Seppuku says gently. "The world demands they carry more than they can bear."

Justice studies the girl again. She's just a child drowning in a weight she never deserved.

For a split second, a face flashes in his mind—Alyssa's—lost, hurting. Did she ever look in a mirror like this? Does she ever feel this alone?

The thought burns and vanishes, but not completely.

Seppuku continues, "She was assaulted by an older boy one year ago tonight. A classmate betrayed her to help the perpetrator and then called her a liar. Her parents believed the lie, not their own daughter. She relives that night—the assault and the betrayal— every time she closes her eyes. Tonight, she wishes only for silence."

The girl raises the knife again. This time, in her mind, it isn't her hand—it's theirs: The classmate's. The boy's. Her parents'. Every cut belongs to someone who failed her, someone who betrayed her.

She slides to the floor, her body folding like paper. Her breath slows. The knife skitters across the tile and settles, stripped of purpose, its blade glinting faintly under the bathroom light.

Justice reaches out, helpless. "She didn't deserve this."

"None of them do." Seppuku kneels beside her and lifts her hand. "Suffering is never balanced—it only transfers. When one soul releases its pain, those who loved her will now bear the weight she laid down."

When the pain finally stops, she exhales—a sound more fragile than breath.

Seppuku kneels, takes her hands, blood and all. "It's time to go."

She looks up, her voice shaking. "Did I do it wrong? Will I suffer?"

"We do not judge," Seppuku whispers. "Your suffering ends here."

He opens the window. A raven lifts from the sill, its wings slicing into the night, carrying the girl's fading light until it dissolves into the dark.

Justice can't look away from the body on the tile.

Seppuku rests a hand on his shoulder. "We are finished here. Come."

The world folds again.

Heat and sound slam into Justice at once—a roaring hum, the tang of exhaust. He blinks through the glare and finds himself on a rooftop surrounded by ventilation units. Gravel crunches underfoot. New York City glitters below.

Again, he wonders at this ability of reapers to move through time and space. He makes a mental note — he must ask about this later.

Seppuku stands at the far edge, watching. Before Justice can take another step toward him to see what has drawn his attention, certainty settles between his shoulder blades—the weight of attention. He turns toward a wall of windows, his focus narrowing to one pane in particular.

Inside, a well-appointed office comes into view. Three figures—two men and a woman—stand motionless, all staring in the same direction as Seppuku. Justice follows their line of sight to a man in a white shirt and tailored slacks balanced on the ledge. His jacket is folded neatly beside him. Only his tie moves, snapping in the wind like a flag.

A single tear slides down the man's cheek.

"When do you see them turn colorless?" Justice asks quietly.

"After," Seppuku answers.

Justice nods slowly. "I've learned something about myself. Sometimes I see what's coming—before it happens. Their future."

"That is… unusual," Seppuku says, studying him. "I see only the moments that lead to choice, not what lies beyond it. This one is a stockbroker. He lost everything— four hundred million dollars of other people's money. Money that belonged to dangerous men, the Triads."

"The Triads, huh?" Justice exhales noisily.

"Hai."

"Then I'm not surprised we're here."

They watch in silence as the man wavers on the edge. Justice closes his eyes for a heartbeat—when he opens them, he and Seppuku are standing on the street below. The wind howls between towers.

The man falls.

Justice can see every detail—the flicker of regret, the panic in his eyes, the helpless twist of his body as it strikes an awning and crumples to the sidewalk below.

The sound is swallowed by chaos. Sirens rise, people scream, phones lift to record the horror.

Justice stands frozen. When he looks again, Seppuku is gone. Across the street, the Reaper kneels beside a gray figure, his raven waiting. A soft caw cuts through the sirens as the soul is taken.

Justice crosses to him. "Can we go back to the roof?"

"No," Seppuku says. "Our task is done."

"But those people I saw behind the glass, the ones that were watching him. They might have driven him to this."

Seppuku's tone remains even. "We do not judge."

"You mean *you* don't judge." Justice's voice hardens. "But I am the Reaper of Justice. Judgment *is* my purpose."

Seppuku studies him a long moment, then bows once and vanishes.

Justice stands alone amid the chaos. "Now what?" he mutters.

He still doesn't understand how to move between worlds. He turns toward the building, ready to try—then suddenly his hand strikes something solid.

The sound echoes—a sharp *clack* on polished wood.

He looks down. The V-shaped table of the chamber gleams beneath his fingers.

Chapter 6: Accident

Expecting to step into the financial building, Justice instead finds himself once again in the chamber. The sight of the familiar walls drains what little energy remains in him. He sinks into his chair at the V-shaped table, folds his arms, and lowers his head onto them.

His thoughts churn—too much information, too many contradictions. The word *moving* flickers through his mind. *Why has no one addressed this with me?*

Then another thought: *three*. The number glows behind his eyes, and he remembers the three figures who had stood watching from the rooftop. *Why are they important?*

He lifts his head and looks around. I've met four Reapers so far. Seven more to go? Will I observe them all the same way?

Even amid confusion, he marvels at how sharply he can recall every encounter, as though each memory has been etched into him. He closes his eyes, focuses on the rooftop scene, and feels the hum of energy gathering. A sudden, deafening *POP!* echoes through the chamber, followed by a sound so unexpected it startles him—a girlish giggle.

Justice's eyes snap open.

Across the table, perched casually in the chair to the left of War's, sits a young woman with flaming red hair and a grin that could start a fire. Her outfit is... alarming—black leather, silver buckles, and boots that climb nearly to her thighs.

She catches his stare, tilts her head, and says with a wink, "Like what you see, sweetie?"

Justice clamps his mouth shut, heat rising to his cheeks, and stares determinedly at the table.

She laughs—a bright, reckless sound. "Relax, I'm only teasing. You Reaper boys are so easy to rattle. Anyway, I am the reaper of accidental deaths—some of the most preventable of the bunch, if you ask me. People trip over their own pride, their own stupidity. No seat belt? *Crash—gone.* Forget to secure a ladder? *Slip—bam!* Like your father-in-law Robert—remember him? Fell off his roof on the Fourth of July."

Justice's eyes widen, but she isn't finished. "Then there are the overdoses—113,000 a year, give or take. Accidents all. Even dear old Mr. Drake Themus, drinking his way to an early grave." She tsk- tsk-ed as she shook her head at him in mock lament.

He straightens, stunned. "What? My death was listed as *accidental?*"

She shrugs, smirking. "Maybe. I didn't reap you, so I can't say for sure. I'm just repeating what I heard."

42

Justice exhales through his nose, wary now. "So you're the Reaper of accidental deaths," he repeats.

"*Ding, ding, ding!*" She claps once, the sound sharp and delighted. "Give the man a prize! Yes, my friends call me Accident. You can too—unless you've got a better name for me?" She winks again.

"Accident is fine." Justice folds his hands on the table. "Why did you mention Robert?"

Her expression shifts, a fleeting softness crossing her features. "Oh, poor thing. It's starting already."

"What's starting?"

"The forgetting." She sighs, theatrically but with an undercurrent of truth. "Earthly memories fade the longer you're here. Honestly, I don't miss mine. Some were *awful.*"

His mind fleetingly floats to his wife, and his daughter, Alyssa. *I don't want to forget my earthly memories*, he muses.

"Not all of them could've been," Justice says, returning to the present. "You sound like someone who's lived a lot of life."

That earns him another grin—this one smaller, almost sincere. "Since you asked nicely…" She sits straighter, pretending to compose herself, though the glint in her eye never quite fades. "As you've probably

43

already guessed, my death was accidental. And you know, stupidity plays its part." Her voice softens a notch. "Let's just say I liked living on the edge. One night, an X-rated game of erotic asphyxiation went too far at the hands of someone less experienced—and well—here I am. Oops." She gestures toward herself with a flourish. "Ta-da."

Justice doesn't know whether to laugh or bow his head. He settles for silence.

"Really?" she says, pouting playfully. "No applause? Tough crowd."

"It's... sad," he admits finally. "But you seem to have made peace with it."

"Peace is overrated." She leans forward, elbows on the table. "I prefer perspective. Death has a sense of humor, Justice. You'll learn that."

He gives a faint smile despite himself. "Are you my next guide?"

"I am. But we've got a minute before curtain call. Want to know more about me?"

"Do I have a choice?" he blurts, then immediately winces. "Kidding. Tell me about the tattoo," he adds, nodding toward her upper arm.

She glances down, and for the first time, her smile softens into something almost reverent. Inked along her bicep is a winged woman with a sword raised skyward.

"This is Kara," she says quietly. "A Valkyrie. She guided the souls of fallen warriors to the afterlife. She's my reminder that there's purpose in the aftermath. My earthly name was taken from her." She traces the outline of the tattoo with one finger, then brightens again. "Anyway, enough about me. Time to clock in."

About that—"

Before Justice can finish the question, he and Accident are standing across the street from a brightly lit car dealership.

Not sure what a car dealership has to do with an accidental reaping, Justice thinks. The thought connects briefly to earlier questions about how travel works in this realm, but before he can dig into it, a massive blast of horns erupts in the distance.

Shouting follows. Music. Then the unmistakable roar of over-amplified exhaust.

Justice looks at Accident. She's already dancing, clapping, clearly enjoying herself as a parade of lifted 4x4 trucks rolls to a stop in front of the dealership. Never in his life—or what he supposes is now his afterlife—has he seen so many trucks, so many flags, so many declarations of loyalty crammed into one place.

As the vehicles idle, a second group emerges from the shadows, spilling into the street with protest signs raised, chants rising fast and furious. They greatly outnumber the truck convoy, but that does nothing to quiet either side. Yelling escalates. Fingers point. Insults fly.

As the two groups press closer, Justice notices movement at the edges of the crowd.

There's a third group.

He taps Accident on the shoulder. "Who are they?"

"They're the party starters," Accident says brightly. "I suppose a word you'd understand better is *hooligans*." She bounces slightly on the balls of her feet, anticipation lighting her face.

As the word sinks in, Justice spots them clearly now—high-pressure paint sprayers slung over shoulders, glass bottles clenched tight, rags stuffed into their mouths. Molotov cocktails.

The air feels charged, electric. Justice knows chaos is coming—and almost on cue, drivers pour out of the trucks, shoving into the front line of protesters.

"Here we go!" Accident shouts, clapping her hands.

"How do you know?" Justice asks. "What did I miss?"

"What you missed," she says, eyes never leaving the crowd, "is that both groups track law-enforcement movement. They all just heard *ICE* on their scanners. The party starters don't know that, though. They're just feeding off the energy."

Justice shakes his head, overwhelmed. "Accident, with every other reaping I've observed, I could tell who it would be. I have no idea what's happening here."

"Oh, sweetie," she says. "I do forget my manners sometimes. As the Reaper of Accidental deaths, I usually get a bit of backstory before I show up. Most of the time, I arrive early. I like to watch... if you know what I mean..."

She flashes him that sickly sweet grin again, eyes dancing as they sweep over the crowd.

"So," Justice presses, urgency creeping into his voice, "who are we here for?"

"Yes, yes, I'll share," Accident says. "What we have here is a political party issue—two opposing sides, both convinced they're right, both convinced the other is the enemy. Protest always brings out the worst in humans."

She gestures vaguely into the mass of bodies.

"We're here for Darlene. She came because she wants to be a voice for change in immigration policy. Her family immigrated here. She's legal herself, but she knows plenty who aren't. She had a run-in with ICE once —it ended favorably for her, but it left her questioning how many people get stuck in a system that's broken." Accident smiles. "Enough for now. Let's just watch."

Her attention snaps back to the street.

P'TING.

SPLAT.

Paint explodes across the sides of the trucks as the hooligans open fire with their sprayers. Shouts erupt. From the back of one vehicle, a thick cloud of mace billows outward, rolling into the crowd.

Coughing turns to panic.

A Molotov cocktail sails overhead.

It hits the ground and bursts into flame—then three gunshots crack through the air.

Chaos is instant.

Accident jumps up and down, clapping wildly. Justice can only stand there, shock etched across his face.

As the situation spirals, a single thought loops through his mind:

This is like watching dominos fall.

Then it happens.

It's as if a veil lifts from his eyes. The crowd blurs —faces, motion, noise—until Justice can see only one person.

Darlene.

People surge in every direction. She stumbles, falls, and doesn't get back up. A heavy boot slams into her ribs. She tries to move, but the effort twists the broken bone into her lung, puncturing it.

Her breaths turn shallow, wet, desperate.

Accident and Justice step closer, standing over her like sentinels as they wait.

A caw sounds in the distance.

Justice looks up just in time to see a large crow descend from the dark sky and settle on Accident's shoulder.

Darlene cries out once… twice… then goes still. Her color drains, turning grey against the pavement.

"You see?" Accident says lightly. "Completely preventable. All yours, my dear *Safe Word*."

The crow caws and takes flight, carrying the woman's faint grey shimmer into the dark.

Justice stands frozen. The smell of smoke and fear thickens the air. Then, faintly—laughter.

He turns. They're back in the chamber. Accident is spinning lazily in her chair, giggling.

"I don't see what's so funny, Accident," Justice says, voice low.

She stops spinning, wide-eyed and innocent. "Who, me? You know what they say—misery *loves* company."

A faint siren wails through the chamber.

Accident claps her hands, grinning. "That's our cue! Let's go, partner. You're going to love this one." She pauses and regards Justice with a look of exasperation. "Or at least I will."

Dense black smoke fills the air. Justice coughs instinctively, though he doesn't need to breathe. Heat presses against him, heavy and suffocating.

Flames lick the frame of a convertible crushed beneath another vehicle. Two bodies inside are barely recognizable through the haze.

Accident inhales deeply, her tone almost wistful. "Ahh... rush-hour carnage. My favorite time of day."

Justice stares at the burning wreckage, dread rising in his chest. "You call this your *favorite* time of day?"

"Sweetie, everyone's got a type," she says, eyes gleaming in the firelight. "Mine just happens to be chaos."

"Excuse me, I need to guide those two before they linger." Off she goes toward the mustang, Safe Word fluttering after her.

Justice turns his gaze to the other vehicles. Firefighters swarm the scene. Metal groans, radios crackle, lights strobe in reds and blues. In a crushed minivan, a family of five struggles to get free. Two children are rushed to ambulances; the parents and older sibling limp away. They are shaken but alive.

Justice moves toward the third car—a sleek BMW idling at the edge of the chaos. The driver pushes open the door, staggers out, and retches onto the pavement. Even now, the sight makes Justice's stomach twist.

Accident rejoins him, wiping soot from her gloves.

"Let me guess," Justice says. "Totally avoidable."

"You betcha—especially this one."

"So why did I need to see it?"

"Because *puke-face* over there—" she points toward the BMW—"this isn't his first time. He'll walk away again with nothing but a few bruises."

Justice frowns. "What do you mean, *not his first time?*"

"He spends his nights drinking at whatever bar still serves him, then slides behind the wheel and drives home like he's got nine lives. Tonight he cut lanes without looking. The mustang swerved—boom. Dominoes. And here we are."

She folds her arms. "Can you go deal with him now before the cops take him away?"

Justice shakes his head slowly. "Can I what?"

"Deal with him. You know, you're Justice," she says simply. Then, catching herself, adds with mock sweetness, "Oops. Right—you're not *active* yet."

"Not active yet?" His voice darkens.

Her grin falters. "Oh well. Maybe next time. I just thought you'd want justice for all those drunk-driver deaths. Like the one that took your Donna, for instance."

Before she can turn away, Justice grabs her arm and yanks her back to face him. His voice drops to a growl. "What do you mean, *not active yet?*"

Accident freezes. For the first time, she looks genuinely afraid. "Wow... you really have no idea how powerful you're going to become. You remind me of your predece—" She stops abruptly as a low, resonant voice fills the chamber.

"Thank you, Accident. That'll be all." says Lord Grim, dismissively. "You may go.

"Justice, we need to head out. Now."

Justice's hand releases her, but his eyes burn with restrained fury. "This conversation isn't finished."

Accident recovers her smile, that impossible gleam returning to her eyes. "Oh, I know, sweetie. After all— who else do we have but each other? Ta-ta for now. Kisses!"

With a wink and a shimmer of light, she's gone.

Chapter 7: Murder

Justice slams his fist on the table. "How?!"

He wants answers—rules, structure, the mechanics behind the magic. Time is a trickster, and so is Lord Grim. He slips between places as if distance doesn't exist, as if every boundary is merely a suggestion. Why is no one addressing this? Surely the others must remember what it felt like to be new... to be lost.

Accident let too much slip. She was careless, and now Justice is left with more questions than footing. Justice paces the Chamber, running through everything he's seen in his last observation sessions, when the floor seems to just drop out beneath him. He's suddenly pressed against the wall of what appears to be a bedroom.

He scans the room. Three Reapers stand near a large bed. And right beside him, silent and immovable, is Lord Grim.

Justice has no idea if the Reapers can sense their presence. Right now, he doesn't care. He glances at Lord Grim, whose eyes are fixed on the trio by the bed.

Without looking at him, Lord Grim says, "Your agitation is loud. Routine will come. Order will come. For now, you remember Elder and Seppuku. The third is the reaper of those that have been murdered. Murder changes form constantly—face, height, gender, even their voice. You've asked for earthly names before. Murder lost theirs long ago, but for your sake, call them Kharon. Now —watch."

Justice stays still. Lord Grim doesn't move either. But the Reapers' voices carry across the room.

"I have watched Mrs. Lee for years," Elder says softly. "She should not suffer the end her husband plans."

"She is MINE!" Murder shrieks. "She is going to be MURDERED!"

"Mr. Lee will die in the act," Seppuku says, calm and low. "Out of love. It is honorable."

"He's killing himself, so he is also mine!" Murder snaps, their voice shifting wildly.

"That is the definition of suicide," Seppuku answers without emotion.

"NO! NO! NO!" Murder screams, each word pitched like an angry child.

Lord Grim steps into the light. "Justice will make the final decision. But first—Elder, give him their history."

Justice moves toward the bed, standing beside Lord Grim. All three Reapers watch him. Elder gives him a brief warm smile before her face cools again. Seppuku doesn't move except for the hand resting on his short sword. Murder fidgets constantly, unable to hold a single form.

Elder clears her throat. "Today is Mr. and Mrs. Lee's seventieth wedding anniversary. Twelve years ago, Mrs. Lee was diagnosed with Alzheimer's. Mr. Lee has cared for her every day as she drifted from him and from their children. The weight of it has been heavy. At ninety-two, he has decided to end her suffering... and his own."

Justice looks at the elderly Asian couple lying side by side on a handmade quilt, dressed traditionally, incense hanging in the air. Mr. Lee whispers something to his wife and kisses her forehead. She closes her eyes. He follows her. He presses his head against hers, ensuring one bullet will end them both.

Justice shuts his eyes.

A pistol cocks.

"Elder," he says quietly, "Mrs. Lee is yours."

Elder touches Mrs. Lee's hand. Her skin turns grey.

The pistol fires.

"Seppuku, Mr. Lee is yours," Justice says, eyes still closed.

Both Reapers summon their ravens. A whirlwind of caws fills the room—and the Lees vanish.

"YOU ARE WRONG!" Murder screams. Suddenly they're in Justice's face, shifting, twisting. "You know NOTHING! You will suffer for this!" Their voice mutates into his own. "I used to *be* Justice."

His eyes snap open.

They're gone. All of them.

Justice doesn't move. There's no point. He'll be pulled somewhere else soon enough.

He closes his eyes again.

Chapter 8: The Abuser

Afternoon light thins into the muted hush of early evening. A stale breeze brushes across a one-story house whose best years are long gone. The once-green lawn has surrendered to neglect, the paint flakes in tired curls, and a few forgotten children's toys sit sun-bleached on the porch. Even the detached two-car garage sags under its own defeat, a late-model Chevy inside with rusted scars and a missing tailgate.

Justice takes it all in from the sidewalk. He knew he'd simply *appear* somewhere again—another abrupt jump in time, another location with no warning. The inconsistency claws at him more and more. If he's expected to mete out "justice," why won't anyone tell him the rules?

"Ready?" Lord Grim materializes beside him, using the question like an announcement.

Justice doesn't hide his frustration. "Ready for what—or who?"

"No other Reapers this time. This one is yours alone. How you choose to interact with the living is up to you. Your only requirement is the soul of the man inside."

Justice frowns. "What do you mean by 'interact'?"

"As the Reaper of Justice, you have abilities the others do not. You can be seen. Heard. You may intervene if necessary. Justice reapings exist to preserve future innocent lives." Grim speaks as if this should be obvious.

Justice clamps down on the spike of irritation. "Some abilities, yes. But I'm missing information, and you know it."

"There will be time later for questions. All you need, you already know."

Justice stares at him. "Really? Because I've never been here, and I don't remember anything about this house."

"It isn't the house you need to remember. It's the man—Marcus. You met him and his wife in the ER." Lord Grim's tone darkens. "Proceed."

And with that, Lord Grim vanishes.

Justice exhales, steadies himself, and crosses the street with a resolve that masks the flicker of doubt inside him. On the porch, he hesitates. *Knock? Walk in?* If he's going to learn the edges of this role, he might as well push them now. He steps forward—and slips through the door as easily as if he were slipping through water.

The moment he enters, the smell hits him: stale beer, sweat, rotting takeout. The living room is an avalanche of garbage—bottles, wrappers, discarded caps.

A hunting show blares on the TV. Marcus lies passed out on a cracked leather sofa, his mouth open in a jagged snore.

Justice's attention drifts to the photographs lining the wall. He steps closer and studies them one by one. Marcus appears in several—smiling beside the woman from the ER, the same two children flanking them: a little boy and a little girl. Everyone looks happy. Whole.

Justice knows better. Photos lie.

He leans in, studying the children more carefully now, and the truth settles uneasily in his chest. Their skin tone doesn't match Marcus's. Not his.

Moving through the room, he finds more framed pictures scattered among the sparse bookshelves. One stops him cold. The same two children grin up at the camera, but this time they stand beside another woman —one who resembles the woman from the ER, only younger. A handwritten note curls across the corner of the frame:

Love, Tia Priscilla.

Justice exhales slowly and his jaw tightens. Your wife is lying in a hospital bed because of you...and you came home to get drunk.

He mutters aloud before realizing it: "Asshole."

Marcus grunts and shifts.

Damn. It dawns on Justice he should've searched the house first. He has no idea where the children are.

Marcus's eyes crack open. "Who the hell are you? How'd you get in here?"

"Where are the children?"

"I ain't tellin' you shit." Marcus pushes himself upright, snatches an empty bottle off the floor, and swings. The bottle passes harmlessly through Justice, smashing against the wall and sending framed photos clattering down. Marcus collapses under them.

"Devon—find the children!" Justice barks, already scanning the hallway. His raven streaks past him, phasing through a padlocked door.

Justice follows, adrenaline threading with something sharper—righteous fury. The muffled crying behind the door detonates it. He rips the padlock free with supernatural ease and throws open the door. A steep stairway descends into darkness.

Marcus staggers behind him, now wielding a chef's knife. He drives it at Justice's back—only to pass through him, lose balance, and tumble headlong down the stairs. Bones crack against the steps before he crumples at the bottom, a greyed, empty husk.

Justice descends, noticing as he does that he can see perfectly in the dark. A single bare bulb hangs above;

he yanks the cord. Pale light spills over Marcus's collapsed body—colorless now, already separating from the flesh.

"Devon—he's not ours," Justice says firmly.

Devon withdraws. Another crow swoops in—a stranger—its feathers darker than void. It snatches Marcus's soul and vanishes. *Safe Word.* Accident's crow.

Justice doesn't have time to process the implications; the children need him.

He moves through the cluttered basement until he finds them at last—two small bodies tied to a pipe, broad silver bands of duct tape covering their mouths. Their eyes are swollen from crying. He frees them with slow, gentle movements.

"You're safe now," he murmurs, lifting them easily. "Close your eyes. We're going upstairs."

They cling to him. Once in the kitchen, both cry out, "Where's Mommy?"

"She's still at the hospital, but she'll be back soon," he says, knowing it's a thin comfort.

Then he remembers the photo in the den. "Should we call your Tia Priscilla?"

Both children brighten. The boy nods. "I know her number. But...where are the other firemen?"

62

Justice blinks, looks down, and sees himself in a firefighter's uniform.

"Don't worry," he tells the boy. "They're on the way. Come outside with me."

They sit together on the porch steps as sirens swell in the distance. When the first police cruiser arrives, Justice slips away, unseen, to watch from the street. Firefighters sweep the house. One lifts the girl into his arms—and Justice freezes.

The firefighter's eyes glow white.

"Well, Murder," Justice mutters. "Good of you to join me."

"Accident will not like what you've done," Murder hisses.

"She'll get over it."

"You know so little."

"And yet you're the one lurking in the dark."

Justice turns toward him. "Explain something to me. Why does that firefighter have white eyes?"

"That is simple." Murder's voice fractures into many. "White eyes appear in the living who are tied to a future justice reaping. If you ever completed even *one*, you would understand. Just know—you need me," Murder begins to fade, whispering through the dissolve.

"You need me. You need me." The sound echoes through the chaos.

Justice watches the space where Kharon vanished —uncertain whether he's being warned…or manipulated.

Either way, he feels the truth settling in him like a weight: Justice is not just something he delivers. It's something he's being shaped into.

Chapter 9: The Arsonist

Snowcapped mountains rise against a sky washed purple, neither dawn nor dusk. Justice stands still, trying to feel the passing of time, but nothing lands the way it used to. Seconds don't tick. Hours don't pull. Time drifts around him like fog—there, but impossible to hold.

Lord Grim once spoke of this. Justice closes his eyes, pulling the memory forward.

"Rest assured that routine and order will fall upon you."

Justice exhales hard. *Not helpful, old man.*

The purple sky deepens into indigo. Pine sharpens the air. A second gust pushes salt across his face—ocean salt. Mountains, forest, coastline...none of it fits anything he remembers in life.

He turns slowly. Houses dot the landscape here, each on an acre or more of thick, shadowed land. Behind him stretches dense forest. In front of him stands a two-story home with a detached garage. Warm gold glows behind the windows. Electric candles flicker in each one, rhythmic and faintly familiar.

He narrows his eyes at them, sensing meaning he can't fully access.

"Did you find what you were searching for?"

Justice turns. Lord Grim stands beside him, hands behind his back, expression unreadable.

"Searching for what?" Justice asks.

"The significance of the candles," Lord Grim replies. "You recognize the gesture but not the reason."

Justice admits, "Yes. I know I've seen them before. But the meaning isn't coming."

"The living enjoy rituals," Lord Grim says, looking toward the house. "This one represents hope. Hope for return. Hope for passage. Hope is flexible."

Justice frowns. "Hope for who?"

"That depends," Lord Grim says. Then his tone sharpens slightly. "Before you bury yourself in questions —allow me to explain why we are here." He gestures at the quiet neighborhood. "This is the childhood home of Tiffany. We are outside Portland, Oregon. She returned home last year to be the full-time caregiver for her mother."

"Is Elder with us?"

"No. This reaping is all yours."

Justice stiffens. "Then tell me why. And why here."

Lord Grim studies him. "Because this path intersects with your last one. You saw a firefighter with white eyes during the assignment with Marcus."

"Yes. Murder said white eyes mean a future reap."

"Not just future. Future *justice* reap," Lord Grim corrects. "And in this case, the firefighter is Tiffany's brother."

Justice's gaze snaps back to the house. "Then why aren't we at *his* place? Why are we here?"

Lord Grim's mouth curves almost imperceptibly. "Because Tiffany is the pivot point. Gilbert—her younger brother—is drowning in divorce costs. In his current financial situation, he risks losing custody of his children and his home."

Justice absorbs that silently.

"To help him, Tiffany intends to create small, controlled fires in Northern California," Lord Grim continues. "In her mind, she will trigger statewide deployment. Overtime. Emergency exemptions. Which will give him extra time before the custody hearing."

Justice feels the gravity settle into his chest. "She thinks she can control wildfires."

"She thinks she can control fate," Lord Grim says. "We are here for you to learn the reach of your abilities—and their boundaries."

Justice nods, though his pulse flickers with unease.

"Now proceed," Lord Grim says, fading into the gathering night.

Justice watches the house again. The candles glow brighter as darkness thickens. His vision blurs—then shifts—as memories he does not own begin pouring into his mind. Scenes. Sensations. Tiffany's days. Tiffany's exhaustion. Tiffany's sense of drowning beneath responsibility.

The world around him slides away.

Tiffany finally gets her mother settled at 9:17 p.m. She eases the bedroom door shut, shoulders sagging as soon as her mother can no longer see her. She slips out through the kitchen door, crossing the gravel easement to the garage with practiced stealth.

Justice follows her inside.

Tiffany locks the door behind her. She doesn't turn on the overhead light—too bright, too risky. Instead, she clicks on her phone flashlight and heads toward a curtained-off corner. She pulls the curtain aside, revealing a small desk lamp and a workspace arranged with quiet desperation.

A topographical map of Northern California spread across the desk.

Red circles marking reservoirs. Highlighted road routes. Ten three-gallon gas cans lined neatly against the wall. A box of flares. A softly crackling police scanner.

Justice steps fully into the room.

She spins, scissors lifted, ready to strike. "Stop! Don't move!"

He raises his hands. "Tiffany, I'm not here to hurt you. My name is Justice, and I'm here to help you."

"Look, Justin…"

"Justice," he corrects her calmly. "My name is Justice."

Her eyebrows twitch upward. "That's worse." She lowers the scissors slightly. "Look, if you're here to sell essential oils or save my soul, I'm not in the mood. My mother finally fell asleep and I have—" she gestures sharply at the map, "—work to do."

"No religion. No sales pitch," he says gently. "Just conversation."

"Hard pass. Goodbye."

Justice tilts his head toward the small old television on the side bench. "Maybe I should show you something instead." The screen flickers to life.

Tiffany startles. Her hand flies to her chest.

Dan Ashley's voice fills the garage: "We interrupt scheduled programming to bring you breaking updates on the developing wildfire situation—"

On the screen:

Flames swallowing mountainsides.

Evacuations ordered across multiple counties.

Death toll rising.

Names of fallen firefighters — Gilbert's name among them.

Tiffany screams as if stabbed. "No—no, no!" She frantically shoves maps aside, patting her pockets for her phone. "I need to call him—I need—Gilbert—"

Justice steps forward slowly. "There's no need to call. He's alive. For now."

She freezes, breath ragged. "Why would you— why would you show me that?"

"Because this is what happens if you continue with this plan." He gestures to the supplies lining the wall.

Her face collapses. "I'm not trying to hurt anyone. I'm trying to *help* him."

"I know," Justice says softly. "You're trying to protect your brother. And you've been protecting your mother. Protecting the whole family, really."

Tiffany's eyes fill. "He's losing everything. His kids. His house. He's a good father. I can't just sit here and watch—"

"And you won't," Justice says.

She looks up sharply. "I won't? What ...?? Then tell me what to do."

He inhales a slow, anchoring breath. "If you continue, you will kill people. Civilians. Firefighters. Even your brother."

She shakes her head in horror. "No—there must be another way—"

"There is," Justice says. "But it requires a sacrifice."

She stares at him until the truth settles on her like the last note of a song. Her voice trembles. "Mine?"

"Yes."

She crumples backward into the chair as if the word physically hit her. Tears slip silently. Her fingers clutch the edges of the desk. "If I die...will it really help them?"

"Your life insurance will pay off Gilbert's debts," Justice says. "He can keep his home. He can keep custody and move here with the children. Your mother will help him. The whole family will be fine."

Tiffany wipes her face. "And no one burns?"

"No one burns."

She nods once—sharp, decisive, heartbreaking.

Without speaking, she begins taking down the maps. One by one. Pulling thumbtacks from the walls. Crumpling marked papers. Tossing them into the trash can. Each movement grows steadier, more resolved.

Justice steps toward the garage door.

Behind him he hears the splash of gasoline on concrete. Then a quiet sob. Then the scratch of a match.

He doesn't look back.

Flames bloom behind him as he walks down the driveway. Sirens begin rising in the distance. The fire devours the garage in a roar of orange and red. Justice stops at the same place he began his assignment, staring up at the house.

The candles in the windows flicker. Glow brighter. Stretch long shadows across the walls.

Hope for a safe return. Or hope for a safe passage.

A slow, mocking clap breaks the night.

Murder steps from the woods, a grin in his voice. "Really, Seppuku? Can't do a reaping without help?"

Justice doesn't turn. "Let me guess—Accident told you."

"Oh, she tells me everything," Murder laughs. "Maybe we should get her a ball gag. Though honestly? I think she'd enjoy it."

Justice faces him. "You're the reason I'm here. So either teach me how to avoid your mistakes—or leave me alone."

"Mistakes?" Murder scoffs. "I made choices. The best I could."

"If they were the best," Justice says softly, "you'd still have a face. And I'd be in Heaven."

Murder's voice fractures into multiple tones. "You in Heaven? Impossible. I had sight once, remember? I know—"

"ENOUGH."

Lord Grim materializes between them, the air vibrating with authority.

Both Justice and Murder fall silent instantly.

Chapter 10: The Nurse: Part 1

The word *"Enough"* still rings in Justice's head long after Lord Grim vanishes. It vibrates like a struck bell, echoing through the Chamber and through him.

What was Murder going to say?

What did he see in my future?

Justice sits in the Chamber, elbows resting on his knees. Murder's unfinished sentence needles him, pricking the back of his mind. The name Annabelle cuts through the static. A nurse's uniform. A retirement facility. Graceful Living.

Justice closes his eyes.

And the world shifts.

He materializes across the street from Graceful Living Retirement Facility, startled immediately by the heat pressing into him. His body feels the temperature the way he used to, yet not entirely—his nerves interpret sensation, but his form isn't bound by it.

He still doesn't understand how any of this works.

A loud caw snaps him from thought. Devon perches high in a palm tree near the entrance, tilting his head as if judging Justice's hesitation.

"Yeah, yeah," Justice mutters. "Head out of the clouds. Figure out why I'm here."

He crosses the lot and moves through Graceful Living's front doors.

The atmosphere feels different from last time—thicker, heavier, as though the heat bleeds inside and settles into the walls. Residents drift through the hallways like slow-moving currents, aimless and weary, many simply doing anything to keep themselves from falling asleep in their rooms.

Justice moves quietly, following a tug he's come to trust. Annabelle. He knows he's here for her.

Rounding a corner, he hears her voice before he sees her.

"Hello, Annabelle! How's your day going?" Mr. Copper calls, leaning on his walker with theatrical flair.

"I wish I was doing as well as you, Mr. Copper," Annabelle replies, brightening instantly. "You're always moving around here so gallantly. That new hip is treating you right."

"It is!" Mr. Copper grins. "Soon I'll take you dancing."

"Ooh, I'm looking forward to that," she says, shaking her hips playfully.

Mr. Copper laughs. "You know what I like."

Annabelle waves and continues down the hall, humming softly. Justice walks with her, observing. Every resident she passes smiles a little brighter. She adjusts blankets. Fixes a button. Brushes someone's hair from their forehead. Each gesture is gentle and practiced.

Justice watches closely for any sign—any mistreatment, any shadow in her behavior. Nothing feels wrong.

During a brief break, she settles behind the nurses' station and begins typing end-of-shift notes. Justice lingers behind her shoulder. She reaches for a new file, flips it open—and her posture shifts. Her shoulders drop. Her breath slows. Sadness shadows her features.

Justice leans in to read.

It's a traveling physician's report.

Patient: *Sabina Minh, age 63.* Eight years in a medically fragile unit after a catastrophic car accident. Husband dead. No children. Mother—her last visitor— passed away three years ago.

Sabina's body has long since forgotten how to function on its own. She cannot create tears, swallow, blink, or even shift her weight. Her skin breaks down faster than the staff can heal it, leaving bed sores that reopen again and again. Her veins are scarred from years

76

of IV lines that cause infection, yet are needed because they provide access to the medications meant to ease a pain no one can measure. Her eyes have been taped shut for so long that the staff no longer remembers what color they are; the coverings are the only way to keep them moist.

She lies in the same bed she has occupied for eight years—neither living nor dying. She is suspended in a limbo that machines maintain with steady, unchanging hums. There is no family left to visit her. No one to speak her name except the nurses who bathe her, turn her, and care for her out of duty and compassion. The lawsuit settlement pays for her existence, but it cannot provide a life.

Annabelle's fingers tighten gently on the edges of Sabina's chart, her face softening in a grief she carries alone. It is clear she isn't reading a patient report; she's reading a reminder of someone caught in suffering so long and so silent that no one but her seems to remember it is still happening.

The report ends with clinical praise for staff diligence and no further recommendations.

Annabelle closes the file gently, pressing her palm against it as if steadying herself. Justice wishes—not for the first time—that he could read minds.

Annabelle rises, adjusts the small leather pouch at her waist, and tells the nurse beside her, "I'm heading to room 105."

Justice follows.

Annabelle enters the code for the "Medically Fragile" ward. Justice recognizes it. He's seen wings like this before. People only leave them one way: under a mortuary sheet.

She enters Sabina's room with familiar tenderness, checking machines, lines, vitals. Monitoring what there is left to monitor.

Justice steps in behind her.

Murder stands at the foot of the bed, as still as a statue.

Without turning, Murder says, "Hello, Justice. Good to see you again."

Justice's stomach tightens. "I'm not sure I can say the same. I assume something bad is about to happen."

"Depends on your definition of bad." Murder's tone has an edge of amusement. "Annabelle here is about to end our dear Sabina's suffering. Want to call Elder?"

Justice frowns. "What are you talking about?"

Murder tips his head toward Annabelle. "Our beloved nurse, adored by everyone on this floor, is about to help Sabina die. Faster. Mercy, compassion... or murder, depending on your views." He grins. "Do you want Elder to handle it? Or will you?"

Before Justice can answer, Annabelle leans close to Sabina.

"Oh, my sweet Sabina," she whispers. "Today is your eighth anniversary with us. I'm finally going to set you free. You deserve to be with your husband and your mother."

She opens the small leather pouch and removes a vial of T31. She draws 5 ml of the liquid into a syringe and slides the needle into Sabina's IV port.

Justice's breath catches.

Annabelle presses the plunger slowly, tears pooling in her eyes.

She kisses Sabina's forehead.

"Goodbye, my dear. No more pain."

Then, softly, "I'm sorry."

She closes the pouch, removes it from her waist, and slips from the room, walking quickly toward the far storage closet.

Justice and Murder stand in stunned silence.

Sabina's chest rises once.

Falls.

Rises again.

Stops.

The room becomes impossibly quiet. Sabina's body turns colorless grey.

Murder breaks the silence first. "Well, I have mine. Are you getting yours? The judgment of justice should be swift, you know."

"Swift?" Justice turns sharply. "That's how *you* acted. There's more to Annabelle than what we just saw. I need—"

"She is a murderer," Murder snaps. "You watched her inject a lethal dose. I wouldn't be here otherwise. Don't pretend there's more to learn. You know so little."

Justice steps back, thinking hard. "You're right. I know almost nothing. That's why I need more information. And Annabelle isn't going anywhere. She still has a date with Mr. Copper."

Murder scoffs.

Justice fixes him with a hard look. "I'm going back to the Chamber."

And he disappears.

A crow caws in the silence.

It swoops in.

Sabina's grey soul is taken.

Chapter 11: Justice Questions

Justice paces the Chamber, each step echoing faintly against stone that doesn't hold sound the way earthly rooms do. Murder's unfinished words keep looping in his head, fraying his thoughts.

You do things…

And then: *ENOUGH.*

Justice rubs the back of his neck. "What should I do?" he asks the empty air.

Devon caws softly. The raven lifts off his perch and glides to Lord Grim's empty chair, landing atop the great scythe that rests against it.

Justice follows Devon's gaze.

"Good idea," he says. "I'll summon him. I need answers."

He approaches the scythe. It hums faintly, a low vibration he feels more than hears. With both hands he tries to lift it—managing only to raise it a few inches before it slips from his grip and settles soundlessly onto the table.

Justice blinks. "Did it…work?"

Devon flutters back to his perch. That's when Justice notices the crack.

A thin black line splits the left side of the table. It creeps forward, widening as it passes each chair on that side—spreading with an almost living intention. A sudden cold floods the Chamber, sharp and crushing, and Justice's breath catches.

The cold is familiar. Cemetery-night familiar.

He feels eyes on him.

Justice turns—and Lord Grim is sitting in his chair, still as stone, watching him.

"You summoned me?" Lord Grim asks.

Justice drops to his knees. "I apologize, My Lord."

"Stand," Lord Grim says sharply. "You work for me. You do not worship me. Now, what do you want?"

Justice rises quickly, heart pounding. "Why did you choose me? How did Kharon go from the Reaper of Justice to the Reaper of Murder? I must know."

Lord Grim's expression doesn't change. "He became unjust."

"How?" Justice asks. "I need to know the whole story. I don't want to follow the same path."

Lord Grim folds his hands on the table. "He is the embodiment of the old saying: *Absolute power corrupts absolutely.*"

Justice feels a pulse of dread. "Was there no counterbalance? Nothing to pull him back?"

"There was," Lord Grim says. "But he refused to listen to her. And the choices he made led to his position now."

Justice's eyebrows lift. "*Her*? Who is she? And does she still hold that role?"

Lord Grim nods. "Her name is Mercy. She is an Eternal—created by God, as I was—in the time before time. During the early years of human existence, I was given the charge to reap on a large scale. Mercy was given the charge to save some. She is the counterweight. The influence of hope during some events."

Justice stares. "…What events?"

"The eruption of Pompeii. The destruction of Sodom and Gomorrah. And the great flood," Lord Grim says calmly. "When judgment fell upon the many, Mercy argued for the few. She always found an exit for the righteous."

Justice's voice drops to a whisper. "Will she appear to me? Will she guide me?"

"She will," Lord Grim says. "But understand this: her guidance is rarely straightforward. Mercy is not law. Her guidance is not rule." His eyes narrow slightly. "Endless mercy can lead to downfall as well. Judgment must still stand."

Justice swallows hard. "The history of the Reaper of Justice... It seems complicated, my lord. Will I be taught the full story? All the ones who came before me?"

"In time," Lord Grim says. "Mercy and I will teach you more as you grow into what you are becoming."

He stands, the Chamber shifting subtly with his movement.

"For now," Lord Grim says, "you go back to work."

And with a blink of darkness, he is gone.

Chapter 12: The Nurse: Part 2

With the promise of Mercy's guidance still echoing faintly in his mind, Justice rematerializes outside Graceful Living Retirement Facility. Devon circles overhead once before settling on the roofline, watching him with sharp eyes.

Justice enters the building with more certainty than last time—but still without a clear understanding of what Mercy expects of him. He senses Annabelle long before he sees her and follows the familiar pull down the hallways.

Annabelle moves through her end-of-day routine with practiced rhythm. She talks softly to a resident who cannot remember her name, straightens a painting on the wall, helps a coworker lift a patient into bed. When she clocks out, she waves goodnight, the kind of gesture that tells everyone she will be missed the moment she leaves.

But she doesn't leave.

Instead of heading toward the exit, Annabelle slips quietly back into the restricted wing, the same hallway where Sabina died two weeks before. Justice feels the weight of that memory settle around them.

Annabelle doesn't enter any rooms—no check-ins, no last-minute tasks. She heads straight for the storage closet at the end of the hall. The one where she hid the vial.

Justice follows her through the door.

The closet is small and dim, smelling of antiseptic and cardboard. Annabelle rummages through shelves, careful, focused, almost anxious. She looks for the vial— not to use it, Justice senses, but to remove it, to erase the evidence of what she's done.

She believes the world has returned to normal— No questions asked. No suspicions raised after Sabina's cremation.

The memorial service was beautiful; she was comforted to see so many people there.

Justice watches her search, wondering how someone who carries so much compassion could be poised at the edge of such a devastating mistake.

A low voice breaks the silence.

"Good evening, death fans!" Murder materializes beside Justice, pretending to hold a microphone. "Welcome to tonight's thrilling episode: *Can Justice reap his first living soul, or will he run away again and let another injustice bloom in this cruel world?* The suspense is unbearable. Truly—you could cut it with a knife."

Murder chuckles. "That's it, actually. Do it with a knife. Very poetic. Come on now my friend, you have so many choices."

Justice doesn't look at him. "Choices? What choices do I really have? I'm a reaper."

"You are Justice," a gentle female voice says. "That means you always have choices."

Justice freezes.

Murder catches the change in his expression and laughs sharply. "Oh, she's here, isn't she? Don't answer—I can see it in that dumb look on your face. Party crasher."

"You can't see her?" Justice asks.

"Nope," Murder says with a smirk. "We ended things. Bad breakup."

Justice turns slowly.

A woman stands near Annabelle, radiant in a way that is not visual so much as felt. Her presence softens the air, bends it toward warmth. Justice feels awe, fear, and relief all at once.

"Justice," she says gently, "you are the only reaper I interact with directly. With the others, I shift circumstances—but I do not appear. You make choices, and I respect them. Mercy is always a choice."

Her presence ripples through him.

Murder groans. "Enough lovebird nonsense. Annabelle isn't going to stay in here all night. Time to do your job."

Mercy glances at Justice and nods once—an encouragement, not a command—then vanishes like a breath of wind.

Justice lets out a shaky exhale. He cannot appear to Annabelle as he is; he knows that now. So he steps back into the hallway and re-enters from the outside, as a doctor would.

As the door swings open, he sees her.

Annabelle stands near the shelf, holding the vial up to the light to check how much remains.

"Annabelle," Justice says, clearing his throat.

She jumps. The vial slips from her hand. She tries to catch it but misses, and the glass shatters on the floor. A shard slices her palm, and a small splash of T31 hits her skin.

Her breath stutters.

She straightens clumsily. "I—I'm sorry, doctor. I didn't hear you come in." She presses her bleeding hand to her chest. Panic flares behind her eyes as she calculates a way out.

Justice steps forward. "Annabelle, I know what that is. And I know what you've done."

Her face goes pale.

He continues, voice steady but gentle. "I offer you two choices. You can seek treatment. That will expose you. You will be judged by human law, punished, and imprisoned—but you will live. Or—" he swallows "—I can take your soul now. Without pain. And you will face your eternal judgment."

Silence fills the space.

Annabelle stares at him—not at a doctor, but at the truth of him. She sees it now, sees *him*, the same way Sabina must have felt his presence.

"I'm... I'm sorry," she whispers. "I don't really understand what's happening. You're asking me if I want to live and go to prison... or die?"

Justice says nothing. He lets the gravity of her choice settle.

Annabelle looks down at her cut hand. Then she grabs a rag from the shelf, wraps it, and walks past him —quick, determined. She heads straight out the door and down the hall.

Justice follows her just long enough to see her leave the facility and walk toward the hospital's emergency entrance.

90

She has made her choice.

Justice steps back into the hall, expecting Mercy to appear with reassurance—some sign that he chose correctly.

But only Murder waits.

Murder smirks. "I can see that disappointment on your face. Waiting for her to pat your head? I remember that feeling. She doesn't stay, Justice. She assumes you'll always do the right thing." His tone sharpens. "But what you did tonight? Not the right thing. You've made an enemy."

Murder vanishes in a hiss of shadow.

Justice breathes deeply, reaching into Annabelle's future. He sees her walk into the ER, report the exposure, and confess everything. When police arrive at Graceful Living, they find the vial's remains, the written statement, and all the evidence exactly as she described.

As the officer seals the items collected from the storage room, two prayer cards slip from the leather pouch—one bearing Sabina's name, the other belonging to a Mr. McMarchesa, who died three years earlier.

Justice stares at the revelation.

Annabelle didn't kill just one person.

She killed two.

Chapter 13: The Plot

Leaving Justice at Graceful Living, Murder materializes in the corner booth of Janing's Pub. The bar is dim and humid, lit by flickering amber bulbs that cast long shadows across peeling vinyl seats. Tracy, the bartender, slides a bottle in front of him, oblivious to the creature he's serving.

Murder ignores him. Rage builds inside them, a tight, pulsing pressure that claws against his hollow form. He digs at the label on the bottle until strips of wet paper cling to his fingers. None of it helps. Justice has gone too far. Justice has *defied* him.

He should see it by now, Murder thinks. *I've shown him everything. Why won't he listen?*

He flicks the bottle cap across the booth in irritation. Why hasn't Accident arrived? He requested her ages ago. She should have felt the pull instantly.

A ripple of warm air crosses the seat across from him.

Accident appears.

"What is wrong with him!?"

Murder erupts before she can even speak. His voice rattles the bottle on the table. "Can he not see the truth right in front of his eyes? He only has to open them. I have shown him *everything*."

Accident's expression softens. She reaches across the table, her hand brushing the edge of his faceless cheek. "I know, my love. We can't control that he doesn't understand your brilliance. You can't rip yourself apart over his shortcomings."

"Shortcomings?" Murder snaps. "He has advanced faster than any of us—faster than I ever did. Do you not remember when he *handled* you?"

Accident smiles faintly. "Oh, I remember. He touched me, commanded me... which, as you know, is my specialty in relationships. With everyone except you." She taps the table. "Justice didn't progress quickly because he's gifted. He progressed because Lord Grim made us drag him around, hand-in-hand, spoon-feeding answers to his endless questions."

Murder snarls. "I remember you taunting him with the drunk driver incident. Your version of 'fun.'"

"I thought you didn't notice," she says with a grin. "That fun created an opening. Something we can use. Perhaps... a way to reach him through his mortal life?"

Murder's rage still simmers, but the curiosity in his posture sharpens. "Perhaps. But I need action now. Justice must suffer *now* for his choices."

Accident cups Murder's head with both hands—tender, affectionate, terrifying. She presses a kiss to the top of his faceless skull. "Justice moves slowly, my love. Punishment moves slowly. We must plant seeds of discontent and nurture them until they twist him. I know it will work. It worked on you, after all."

Murder shudders, delight mixing with fury. "You are quite the bitch," he says sweetly.

Accident beams. "Thank you."

Murder leans forward. "These... seeds. How do we create holes to plant them?"

"A hole," Accident says thoughtfully, "can be made by protecting someone on his list. Someone he hasn't met. Someone whose survival shifts the balance."

Murder straightens, energized for the first time since entering the pub. "Yes. Yes, of course. Someone on his reaping list." A wicked smile creeps across the blank plane of his face. "I know just the man. Khadir al-Bashir —the warlord."

Accident's eyes glitter. "Perfect."

"Justice expects him to die," Murder says. "If we protect him, the chaos will ripple. It will confuse him. Undermine him. Hurt him."

Accident clasps her hands together with delight. "You seem happier already!"

Murder lifts the torn beer label and flicks it away like a piece of ash.

"Oh, I am," he says. "At last—we have a plan."

Chapter 14: Warlord

The restless energy that has gnawed at Justice since Annabelle's reaping finally begins to ease. The moment he materializes inside the Chamber of Entrance, he notices it again—empty. Always empty. No other Reapers, no activity, no movement.

It bothers him more each time.

He tries to recall the number Lord Grim gave him —the staggering count of human deaths per minute... or was it per second? With billions alive, why does this place feel abandoned?

As Justice turns this over in his mind, a ripple of heat rolls through the Chamber. War appears.

Justice smirks. "A moment of rest?"

War booms a laugh. "Not since the day I was created. And you—how is *your* war going?"

"Is that what we're calling it now? 'War'?"

"Of course." War stretches, the metal clasps on his armor clinking lightly. "Good versus evil. Left versus right. Accident has been fluttering between everyone, talking and talking. And I must say—" he nods toward the long ceremonial table "—I do enjoy the crack on the left side. Very dramatic. Though why not the right?"

Justice sighs. "It wasn't my finest moment. Can I ask you something?"

"No, I am not a vegan," War says, erupting into a deep belly laugh.

Justice chuckles despite himself. "Good to know. But that's not it." He grows more serious. "Why do you sit on the left side of the table with Murder, Accident, and Disease? Our interactions have been… positive. You've helped me. You have a sense of humor."

War dips his head graciously. "Thank you. But I sit on the left because war itself cannot be classified as good. Physical force taken to gain resources, land, revenge— that is my domain. The necessity of violence keeps me on this side."

Justice nods slowly. "I suppose that makes sense. But something else has been bothering me since we met." He pauses. "It's Khadir al-Bashir."

War goes still. "You may confide in me."

"I can't find him," Justice says. "I've foresighted him twice. Both times, when I arrive, I see *you* reaping others—but he's gone. Vanished. He's on my list, but I can't reach him. It makes no sense."

War lets out a long breath. Then he gives a crooked smile. "It makes perfect sense, actually. But tell me—why don't you know the answer?"

Justice stiffens. "What answer?"

War leans in, grin widening. "Murder is protecting Khadir al-Bashir. Every time you locate him, Murder rushes to warn him. The warlord inflicts the damage meant for his destiny, then flees before you arrive."

Justice's jaw drops. "You're kidding me. Why would that be allowed?"

"No joke," War says. "I know you enjoy my humor, but not this time. Khadir al-Bashir is one of Murder's favorites because he killed his own predecessor. And Murder hates you, Justice. Truly hates you. He despises the way you work. His little game forces *me* to clean up all the carnage while he hides his champion."

Justice rubs his forehead. "Can he be punished for this?"

"He already was," War replies. "He lost his face for the ultimate act. And besides—who would want to inherit Murder's mantle?"

"Would Accident want to be the Reaper of Murder if he's removed?"

War snorts. "She'd like being second most powerful, yes... but she'd never give up that leather outfit." He smirks knowingly.

Justice steels himself. "War, would you help me complete the reaping of Khadir al-Bashir? Saying yes pits you against your entire side of the table."

War sits forward, intrigued. "Go on."

"My plan comes from the Bible," Justice says. "Mark 13:7–8."

War's eyes spark. "Rumors of wars." He taps the table. "Deceivers. Uprisings. I like it. How can I help?"

"Murder and Accident are too suspicious of me to fall for anything I say. But you—" Justice gestures toward War's armor "—they trust you. If you start a rumor about a new outbreak of war, Accident will rush to tell Murder. Murder will insist that Khadir al-Bashir be present at the location. And I will be waiting. No time for escape. No time for protection."

War laughs—loud, delighted. "I will help. And I will let you know where to be." He cracks his neck. "Besides, I could use a little time off."

War leans back in his chair to catch his breath. Moments later, Accident pops in—loud, chaotic, smiling as if the Chamber belongs to her.

She lands in her chair with a bounce.

War opens one eye. Accident's face is inches from his.

Perfect.

War seizes the moment. He whispers news of an impending battle—one with weapon caches, unclaimed territories, and enormous potential for death.

Accident squeals with excitement and vanishes to fetch Murder.

Murder arrives soon after. Accident breathlessly recounts the rumor—fresh war, fresh profit, fresh chaos. Murder's posture loosens.

Of course Khadir al-Bashir would be there.

He must be there.

Deep in the desert, Khadir al-Bashir stands before a makeshift tent marked on his map. The promise of stolen anti-tank and anti-air missiles lures him forward; these weapons will secure his rise, crush his rivals, and place him above every warlord in his path.

He orders his men to kill the guards.

They comply.

Inside the tent, crates are stacked neatly, just as War described. Khadir smiles, stepping close—

Justice materializes in front of the crates.

Khadir freezes.

"No!" he shouts. "I am protected from you! I was told you could never take me!"

"I'm sure you struck a deal to be protected from me," Justice says calmly. "But I'm not here for you."

Khadir's confusion swells into terror.

"I'm here," Justice says, "to introduce you to another Reaper."

Behind him, the air distorts, thickens, rots.

"I would like you to meet the Reaper Disease."

Screams erupt as Disease's presence fills the tent.

Men collapse, convulsing. Skin sloughs from bone. Blood pours from eyes, ears, mouths. Khadir al-Bashir clutches his throat as sores rip across his body.

The tent becomes a chamber of agony.

Justice watches.

Silent.

Unflinching.

The warlord's screams are the last to fade.

Chapter 15: Call to Order

Justice steps into the Chamber of Entrance—and stops cold. Murder is sitting in his chair with his feet up on the table and his arms behind his head like he owns the place.

"You asswipe!" Justice snaps.

Murder sits up, indignant. *"Me?!* You reaped someone under my protection. I had a deal with him!"

"As much as you want to pretend you're Lucifer, you don't get to make deals for the souls of the living," Justice fires back. "You'd think losing your face would've taught you not to pose as something higher than the rest of us. Now get out of my chair."

Murder slides off the seat with a theatrical sigh. "Fine. I'll move. This whole side of the table disgusts me anyway—so self-righteous and pretentious." He drags his fingers along the crack splitting the left edge of the table as he walks around to his own chair.

Justice crosses his arms. "Sounds more like jealousy than disgust. Weren't you over here once?"

"Yes," Murder says sharply. "And I left by choice. Unlike the rest of them. Elder and Lullaby have it so easy —nature takes its time, no fuss. Even Seppuku, all dramatic and tragic, tries to call it honorable. Lying to oneself is pathetic." He leans forward. "Speaking of lies —when are you going to stop hiding behind the others and do your own reaping?"

"Oh, boo-hoo," Justice says. "The souls were reaped. Judgment was delivered. Everything proceeded as it should. You're still crying because I used Disease and ruined your little warlord deal. Khadir al-Bashir is exactly where he belongs—meeting Lucifer face-to-face."

Murder flips him off. "You're so tricky."

Justice smirks. "I learned something from you."

Murder leans back. "Then let's settle this—for good. How do you want to do it?"

Justice doesn't respond. He walks to the head of the table and places his hand on Lord Grim's great scythe.

Murder laughs. "What's that for? Gonna crack the other side of the table?"

A cold rush sweeps the Chamber.

Lord Grim appears in his chair. "That won't be necessary."

Both of the Reapers bow their heads.

Justice and Murder say together, "Yes, Lord Grim."

"I will hear both sides," Lord Grim says. "And I will decide—and set new standards if needed. Murder, you may begin, since you claim offense."

Murder stands. "Simple. That... creature—" he gestures at Justice "—who pretends to be the Reaper of Justice has not reaped a single soul. Even when assigned directly by you."

Lord Grim nods. "Justice, your counter?"

Justice meets his gaze. "Every soul assigned to Justice has been judged and collected. If not by my hand, then by another Reaper acting within their role— Accident, Disease, Seppuku. Their categories fit the situation. The end justified the means, if we're using non-scriptural standards. And Annabelle—she chose her earthly judgment herself."

Murder's laugh is sharp. "You sound like a Nazi officer at Nuremberg. Humans marched into gas chambers because someone 'followed orders.' That's your defense?"

"I followed the example set by our Lord," Justice says calmly. "He uses all of us to carry out tasks. He could reap every soul himself, but he values our styles."

Murder slams his hand on the table. "We use our *own* talents. You only know how to use *us*. You haven't shown any talents or styles of your own."

Justice bristles. "You would have seen my talents if you hadn't interfered with Khadir al-Bashir."

"Interfere?" Murder scoffs. "You let Mercy interfere in your reaping of Annabelle—the murderer."

A shudder ripples through the Chamber.

Lord Grim strikes the floor three times with his scythe.

Mercy materializes at his right.

"Lady Mercy," Lord Grim says, "you are accused of interfering."

Mercy steps forward. "My dear Reapers, I touch every life on Earth. Mercy knows no boundaries. I assist every justice reaping where mercy is needed—just as I did when Murder himself was Justice."

"Thank you, Lady Mercy," Lord Grim says. "I find no fault. You may remain if you'd like."

"I will stay," Mercy replies. "I suspect I'll be needed again."

Justice bows slightly. "Thank you, Lady Mercy, for caring for me in life—and in death."

"Kiss a—" Murder begins, but his mouth snaps shut violently.

"Murder," Lord Grim warns. "Never again in my presence. Or you will lose your voice next. State your next point."

Murder works his jaw until it opens. "Yes, my Lord. I request you summon Accident. She was the first used by Justice—to reap Marcus the child abuser."

Lord Grim taps the floor once.

Accident bursts into the Chamber. "Oh my! Hello everyone!" she chirps.

Murder points at her. "Did Justice use you to reap Marcus? Did he let him 'accidentally' break his neck?"

"Yes!" Accident says cheerfully. "It was so dramatic! Those poor kids—"

"Only 'yes' or 'no,' please," Lord Grim cuts in. "Take your seat."

Accident curtsies and sits.

"Justice?" Lord Grim asks. "Your counter?"

"Yes. Please summon Seppuku."

A tap of the scythe. Seppuku appears, serene and still.

Justice bows. "Seppuku, when Tiffany—in the burning garage—chose suicide over being taken, her choice summoned you. Did this offend you?"

"No," Seppuku says simply.

"Thank you."

Murder huffs. "Of course he sides with you. You gave him Mr. Lee. This is going nowhere."

Lord Grim lifts the scythe. "The only remaining Reaper involved is Disease."

A ripple of dread precedes Disease's arrival. Metal mask gleaming, presence suffocating.

"I will ask one question," Lord Grim says. "Point to whom you agree with. Words from you would devastate the world."

"Disease, come to our side!" Murder says desperately.

Justice speaks softly. "The side of the table doesn't matter. You can still choose what's right."

Disease surveys them all.

Then raises both arms.

And points equally to both.

Lord Grim nods. "Accepted. Take your seat."

The remaining Reapers—Elder, Lullaby, War—appear in their places. Silence falls.

Lord Grim places his hand on the cracked left side of the table.

The fissure closes slowly, sealing itself until the table is whole once more.

He rises.

"I have decided to honor both requests."

All Reapers murmur: "Both?"

"Murder is correct," Lord Grim says. "Justice—you must complete your next reaping personally. And immediately. All Reapers will remain here until your Raven brings the soul."

Murder grins. "Victory!"

Justice straightens. "And my request?"

Lord Grim meets his eyes. "Upon your return, Mercy and I will answer your question." He lifts the scythe. "Now go."

Chapter 16: The Drunk Driver

The words of Lord Grim follow Justice out of the Chamber like a verdict he can't escape.

"Justice, you must complete your next reap immediately by yourself. All others will stay here until your Raven does the transportation of the soul you take."

Justice shakes his head as if he can dislodge the echo. It doesn't work.

He already knows where he's going. No foresight needed.

Janing's Pub.

He materializes in the alley behind it, the heat of the day clinging to the brick. A battered BMW sits crooked against the wall, and Justice recognizes it instantly. He walks past, running his hand along the dented fender. The car still bears the scars from the night it sideswiped the Mustang and sent it flying into the family van.

One man, so much destruction.

He still doesn't understand how this car runs—or how its driver is free.

Justice heads for the front door, anger simmering under his ribs. *He should be in a jail cell, not a bar.* But when your older brother is a hotshot criminal lawyer, you can apparently buy your way out of anything, even when someone dies.

Or when someone is about to.

Justice doesn't need foresight to know who he's here for. He's already seen this man twice. Foresight only adds one more detail now: the teenage girl from the last crash won't survive the night.

He pushes open the door.

The usual hum of Janing's wraps around him—low music, clinking glass, stale beer and disappointment. Behind the bar, Tracy is moving with his practiced, half-bored efficiency.

Justice takes a seat next to a man who is clearly drunk, hunched over his glass.

He lifts a hand. Tracy notices.

"What can I get'cha?" Tracy asks, sliding down the bar.

"A double Johnnie Walker Blue," Justice says.

"Coming right up." Tracy reaches for the top shelf.

"Top shelf hooch," the man beside him slurs as Tracy sets the drink down. "That's where the good stuff lives."

Justice glances over. Hunter. Same face. Same entitled smirk.

Justice nudges his own glass toward him. "Make that two," he says to Tracy.

Tracy shakes his head. "Ok, but no more for him." He pours a second double and sets it in front of Justice.

Hunter grins. "Thank you, my friend. Didn't catch your name."

"Drake," Justice says easily. "What do your friends call you?"

"Anything, as long as they're buying." Hunter chuckles at his own joke. "Name's Hunter. What brings you to this lovely establishment, Drake?"

He doesn't wait for an answer. His words tumble out fast and slightly slurred.

"There are much nicer places you could be throwing back thirty-dollar shots."

"Yes," Justice says. "But I'm here on business."

Hunter leans in, eyes narrowing. "Oh yeah? What kind of business?"

"Collections," Justice replies.

Hunter studies his face. "You hound people for money?"

"No," Justice says. "Nothing that glamorous." He tilts his head. "Why? Do you owe?"

"Me? No way. I come from old money." Hunter sits up a little straighter, pride dripping off every syllable. "Money will never be an issue for me."

Justice rolls his eyes. "Old money, huh? Then what brings you to this… 'lovely establishment'?"

Hunter laughs and sweeps his gaze around the bar. "Yeah, this place is great, right?" He lowers his voice. "My hotshot attorney brother has me lying low at that fleabag motel across the street."

"Interesting way to describe your situation," Justice says. "Lying low. You in some kind of trouble?"

Hunter looks down at his glass, giving it a swirl. "Nah. Joseph—that's the hotshot brother—says I need to 'cool off' after my little fender bender."

He raises his glass. "Here's to lying low and lovely establishments."

Justice lifts his own. "Here's to us, and all those like us. Damn few left. Bottoms up."

They tap glasses and knock back the whiskey in one swallow.

Hunter sighs. "Now *that's* fine whiskey. Bartender! Another round. Put it on my new friend Drake's tab."

Tracy walks over, shaking his head. "Sorry. You're done. It's your lucky night your 'pal' here shared one, but I'm not serving you anything else. Time for you two to move on. I don't need your 'hotshot' brother coming in here cleaning up after another 'little fender bender.'"

Hunter lunges, fingers curling. "Listen, you—"

Justice grabs his arm firmly. "Come on, man. I don't have a hotshot brother. Let's head to your place. It's just across the street, right?"

Hunter glares at Tracy, but the fight drains out of him. "Right. Screw this place. Plenty of other bars happy to take my money." He slides off the stool, wobbling, and lurches toward the door.

Justice follows him out.

In the alley, Hunter staggers to the BMW and starts patting his pockets. "Where the hell are they?"

Justice steps closer. "Lose something?"

"The keys, genius." Hunter dumps his pockets onto the hood.

"I thought we were going back to your room," Justice says.

"That shithole?" Hunter snorts.

"I thought we agreed the place didn't matter," Justice says, moving a little closer. "And I'm tapped out. Pretty sure you are too."

Hunter looks up and finds Justice right beside him. "What? Kiss my ass. Don't drag me into your quitter life choices. I'm good. Now get out of my way."

"I think you should call it a night," Justice says quietly. "Sleep it off in your room. Or you might actually have to pay this time."

"Ha!" Hunter barks. "I told you. Old money. There's nothing money can't buy. Dear old Dad drilled that in—may he burn in hell." He finds the keys and jabs them toward the lock. "Now get in the car and we'll have a night you'll never forget. Or get the hell out of my way."

Justice opens the passenger door and slides in. "Oh, I won't forget this night," he murmurs.

Hunter drops into the driver's seat, buckles in, and starts the engine. The car coughs, then settles into a rough idle.

"I see you've come to your senses," Hunter says, grinning. "I know the perfect spot."

"Before we go," Justice says, turning toward him, "I have a question."

Hunter squints. "What now?"

"Do you remember how your car got so messed up?"

Hunter's expression hardens. "What does that have to do with anything?"

Justice watches him carefully. "I'm curious if you even know that you sent a teenage girl to the hospital. She's fighting for her life while you're 'cooling off.'"

Hunter shrugs. "So what."

Justice exhales slowly. "So what," he repeats. "In about an hour and ten minutes, that teenager will die from the injuries you caused while driving drunk." His voice drops, steady and cold. "She'll be in Heaven. You, on the other hand, will already have spent an hour in Hell."

Justice places his hand flat on Hunter's chest.

Heat blooms under his palm—then surges. Hunter gasps, clutching at the steering wheel as his body temperature spikes. Sweat pours down his face, then his skin flushes an angry red. Every pore, every vessel betrays him as the heat turns to something unbearable.

Flames erupt, not from outside, but from within. They lick through his clothes, race along his limbs, engulf him. Hunter tries to scream, but the sound chokes off as the fire consumes him.

Justice opens the passenger door and steps out of the car as the blaze roars higher.

He doesn't look away.

When it is done, he lifts his face to the night sky.

"Devon."

A low whoosh circles the burning BMW. Devon materializes briefly in a sweep of black wings and then dives into the wreckage, coming out as a dark streak that shoots upward and vanishes into the sky.

"Take him where he belongs," Justice says softly. "It's been a long night. I'm ready to go home."

Chapter 17: History of Justice

As promised, Lord Grim and Mercy wait in the Chamber when Justice returns from his solo reaping. The exhaustion sits heavy in his limbs; it's not physical fatigue, but the kind that sinks deeper, into memory and conscience.

He just wants to sit down, but Mercy is occupying his seat.

Unsure of the etiquette, Justice hesitates. Devon swoops in through the high arch, circles once, then settles on his perch. Justice looks to Lord Grim for direction.

"Sit anywhere," Lord Grim says. "We can begin."

Justice drops into the nearest chair.

Lord Grim rests his hands on the table. "We arrive at a question with no clean answer: is reaping a human soul for the 'greater good' justifiable?"

The Chamber feels colder as he continues.

"Humans punished wrongdoers before they recorded their own history. Sometimes it took only one voice calling an act 'wrong' for the masses to stone, hang, or behead. By today's standards, many of those deaths would be unjust. Mob mentality ruled. Look at the disciples of Jesus—they spoke against corrupt leaders, and the mobs silenced them."

Justice shifts. The weight of Alyssa slips into his thoughts—how he used to warn her about people in power who hid cruelty under authority. He never wanted her to face a world where justice was twisted by majority opinion. He never wanted *this* path for her father.

Lord Grim continues, unaware of the ache behind Justice's eyes.

"As humanity grew, chaos grew with it. Laws formed. Systems developed. Punishments evolved— electrocution, injection, firing squad, gas. Humans tried to build a structure that protected the innocent and punished the guilty. But all systems fail. Some escape justice. Others are punished unfairly."

Justice thinks of Hunter in his BMW. He thinks of the teenage girl whose parents will soon wake to a nightmare, and of how the human system let Hunter walk free—twice.

Lord Grim's tone deepens. "Those who cause death through disregard must be held accountable— either by the system humans created or by mine. When Murder was Justice, they reaped over sixteen thousand individuals. The Reaper of Justice has... different abilities. Those who fall outside the categories of Accident, Disease, Elder, Lullaby, or Seppuku often fall to Justice."

Mercy watches Justice carefully. He feels it—the concern, the warning, the hope.

"The grey area between killing and justice," Grim says, "is very small. Murder lost the ability to see any good in those assigned to them. They stopped listening to Mercy. They found pleasure in the reaping itself, aligned with Accident, and followed their thrill-seeking urges."

Justice murmurs, "Can they not be replaced? To stop the cycle?"

Lord Grim sighs. "It has been considered. It would not work. Those who can stomach the roles of Accident or Murder—who can endure the ugliness, tolerate the chaos—are rare. They thrive in their positions. Therefore, they are given a wide berth of tolerance. When Murder failed to recognize good, he lost the mantle of Justice and became Kharon, the journeyman through the darkness of murder."

Justice's voice softens. "What made me different? Why choose me?"

"Your earthly faith in the Almighty," Lord Grim answers. "Your moral compass. Your internal struggle to do what is right even when it costs you. We expect you will thrive in this role, just as Accident and Murder thrive in theirs."

Justice absorbs that, uncertain whether it comforts or burdens him. Alyssa's face flickers in his mind again— her smile, her relentless belief that he tried his best even on his darkest days. He wonders if she'd approve of the man he is now… or the being he's becoming.

He asks softly, "What will keep me from becoming like them?"

Mercy steps forward. "If I may, Lord Grim?" At his nod, she continues. "We saw the rise in homicides and fewer acts of justice. So when a new Justice was chosen, Lord Grim became more present—giving guidance, clarity, direction. He ensures the reaps done in the name of justice are intentional, not impulsive. That is why you feel him near."

Justice asks his last question carefully. "If I had refused this role… would I have gone to Heaven?"

Lord Grim's expression is unreadable. "We do not judge. We do not know."

The Chamber fades.

Justice is pulled—not by duty, but by instinct—to Janing's Pub. The moment he steps inside, Tracy waves from behind the bar.

"Hey, man. I remember you from last week. That guy who—what was it—set himself on fire in the alley?"

Justice puts on a weary smile. "Yeah. Crazy night. Sometimes weirdos find me."

"Oh, really?" Tracy nods toward the corner booth. "Speaking of weirdos... that guy over there said he was waiting for someone who only buys good whiskey."

Justice follows his gesture. A hooded figure sits alone.

"Thanks," Justice says.

He approaches the booth.

Murder—Kharon—lifts his glass. "Nice to see you again, Drake. I just want to talk."

"I don't want trouble, Kharon," Justice says. "Will this be civil?"

"Of course." Kharon lifts the second shot glass. "What was the toast Hunter said? Ah, yes—'Here's to us, and those like us.'"

They clink glasses.

The whiskey burns, but Kharon grimaces. "Disappointing. Almost as disappointing as beating you in the Chamber."

"That's because you bought cheap whiskey," Justice replies.

"Perhaps." Kharon leans back. "But I can give you something of value. Grim and Mercy told you the official story of Justice. Now let me give you something more personal."

Justice tenses.

Kharon's voice lowers. "You should take a look at your own future. Drake Themus, the mortician—you think his story ended when yours did?"

Justice's breath catches.

Kharon stands, adjusts his hood, and walks out of the pub.

Leaving Justice with a fresh dread twisting beneath his ribs.

Leaving him wondering what he isn't seeing.

Leaving him thinking—again—of Alyssa.

Chapter 18: Friends Close & Enemies Closer

A shaft of late-afternoon light slips through the door as it swings open at Janings Pub. The beam glints off Tracy's glasses, drawing his attention from the register.

"Welcome in," he calls—then squints. Recognition sparks. "Should've figured you were here for your buddy. Man buys a whole bottle of Johnnie Walker Blue, next thing I know he's got more weirdos showing up."

"You should be careful with comments like that," Kara lilts, stepping inside with a pirouette of her hips. "You never know when a little accident might happen."

Drake hears her voice and waves them over. Kharon strolls beside Kara, all swagger and shadow, and the two slide into the booth opposite Drake.

"To what do we owe the pleasure?" Kharon drawls, already reaching for the bottle. "Can't be out of the goodness of your heart. Or just to buy us a shot."

Drake leans back, steady. "Consider this a courtesy call. We're going to be working together."

Kharon arches a brow. "So you did take my advice. Using that foresight of yours now."

"I hate giving you the satisfaction," Drake mutters, "but yes. Foresight is how I know the three of us will be involved."

"Oh, goodie!" Kara claps, bouncing lightly on the bench. "Teamwork! Group project energy! I love this!"

"We'll be working with Keres too," Drake adds. "Reaper of Fear."

"Girl *power*," Kara squeals, twirling a strand of hair.

Kharon sighs. "Are you going to share the actual vision, or do we have to play Twenty Questions?"

Drake nods. "When I watched Seppuku's reaping, I spotted a future one—three silhouettes on a rooftop. I followed the thread. They're executives from the brokerage that handled the jumper. I know one dies by murder. Another by accident. And the third…" He lets the sentence settle.

Kara gasps. "Oh! Speaking of accidents—BRB!" She blows an exaggerated kiss and vanishes.

Silence drops like dust.

Kharon exhales, the kind that says *finally*. "While she's gone—let me be clear. I don't buy your neat little explanation, not fully. But I'll play along. Encourage her to play along. And when this teamwork is done?" His eyes harden. "I expect the truth."

Drake extends a hand. "Deal."

They shake—firm, careful, a pact between two predators who don't trust each other but need each other all the same.

Kara reappears in a shimmer of pinkish light. "Whew! Okay, picture this: a military funeral, rifles for the salute, *one guy* didn't tighten the flash suppressor and —boom! Headshot. Wild, right? Anyway! What did I miss?"

"Nothing," Drake says, sliding out of the booth. "Kharon will fill you in."

Kharon lifts the nearly empty bottle in a small salute. "Thanks for the good whiskey, Drake."

He downs one last shot. Kara giggles. And in a blink, they both vanish, leaving Drake alone with the echo of their exit and the faintest scent of gunpowder and perfume.

Chapter 19: The Three Executives

Jessica sits motionless at her desk, staring at her forearm. The words *Why Not Me?* blur, sharpen, and blur again as her eyes refocus. The same phrase gleams from the plaque on her desk, catching a sliver of sunlight. The echo of that mantra pulls her backward in time.

Graduation day. UNLV. Jessica stands at the podium in a crimson gown, delivering her commencement speech. When she finishes, she lifts her arm, showing the tattoo to the sea of classmates. The crowd erupts in a rhythmic chant—*Why not me? Why not me?*—as she steps offstage, radiant with certainty.

Now, in her office high above Manhattan, she whispers the words to no one. "Why not me?"
She already knows the answer. They're coming for her—FBI, regulators, investors, maybe worse. The story of their "jumper" has hit every major network, each one speculating about fraud, negligence, and scapegoats. Jessica knows how fast that kind of fire spreads.

But the FBI isn't what worries her most.
It's the foreign investors—the quiet, serious men whose approval she has never once taken lightly. The ones Samuel insisted were "partners." She knows now they are something else entirely. And they do not tolerate chaos.

Her mind slips backward again. *How did I get here?*

She sees Vegas—cheap carpet, neon shadows. Her teenage mother dealing cards to keep them afloat. Jessica studying under flickering lightbulbs, swearing she would build a different life. Graduating valedictorian from UNLV with double majors. Then New York, the NYU finance master's program, the internship where she outpaced every other recruit, her algorithms catching the attention of the C-suite.

And Samuel Amand.

Twenty years older. Silver spoon, smug grin. He thought he was her mentor. She always thought he was a bit of a creep. But he offered her a fast track, and later, when he left to form his own firm, he dragged her upward with him. CEO at thirty-two. Access, prestige, a view from the 33rd floor that made her feel untouchable.

Until now.

"Your statement ready?" Samuel's voice bursts into her office, jarring her back to the present. "Press wants something by five."

"Yes, it's ready," Jessica says, though exhaustion weaves through her tone.

"That's my girl." He grins. "Just make sure Mr. Hi-Tao approves it first."

"Yes, I know the drill," she says, exhaling sharply. "He's in his private lunch. I'm not allowed to disturb the Great Oracle of the Boardroom."

Samuel chuckles. "He has his quirks."

Jessica's eyes narrow. "Do you remember after my mother's funeral, when you offered me the CEO chair? You told me the crown was heavy."

"I said something wise and fatherly, I'm sure."

"No," she counters, "you said you'd already sold your soul years before. And you wanted to give me 'a chance to drive.'"

Samuel waves the thought away. "Details, details."

Jessica watches him leave, her mind spiraling. This isn't going to blow over. They won't accept one pawn removed from the board. They'll want reciprocity. They always do.

She calls her assistant. "Crystal, meet me in my office."

Crystal enters moments later, concerned. Jessica hands her the press statement.

"I need you waiting outside the boardroom. When Mr. Hi-Tao finishes his lunch, give him this to approve. Then text me immediately."

128

"Why your cell? You're leaving?" Crystal asks.

"You're my anchor, Crystal. The only person I hired myself. I trust you. Trust that I know what I'm doing." Jessica forces a reassuring smile. "We have grief counselors the rest of the week. Just… follow my instructions."

Crystal nods reluctantly and leaves.

Jessica stands, straightens her office, takes her blazer, and quietly slips out. Not to the executive elevator —but the public one. She presses P3.

When the doors open, she moves down the cold corridor toward the restricted server room, swiping through the security doors.

Charlie looks up from his post. "Ms. Aguilera! Haven't seen you down here since before you were CEO."

"Has it really been that long?" she says, smiling warmly. "Policy check-in. After today's events, I need to verify all systems are secure."

"Of course. Everything should be in order."

Jessica enters the server core, chill prickling her skin. At the main terminal she slips a flash drive from her shoe and plugs it in. Her fingers fly over the keys.

"Yeah, Daddy Warbucks," she mutters under her breath. "Maybe you forgot I built half of this infrastructure myself."

Encrypted folders open. Communications stream in. Translations load.

Then she sees it.

"King Taijitu can live with one head."

Her breath catches. Her vision blurs.

"They want one of us," she whispers. "One head of the two-headed snake."

She wonders who they'll choose.
She wonders who Samuel has already offered.

She deletes the files, hides the flash drive, and walks out as calmly as possible.

Back at the elevator lobby, her phone reconnects. Notifications explode.

Crystal: *What you asked is done.*

Samuel: *Dinner tonight? Need to talk.*

Others: board members, attorneys, hedge fund partners—she deletes them all unread.

She texts Crystal: *Do you still have the Xmas gift from 3 yrs ago?*

Yes.

Where?

090295

Then she texts Samuel: *Friday. Boardroom. 30th floor.*

Perfect.

See you then.

Two days pass. The building returns to its cold routine. The sidewalk is scrubbed clean. Vendors return. People pretend normal is possible again.

By 7 p.m., the floors are empty.

Jessica answers her office phone.

"Still on for tonight?" Samuel asks.

"Of course. And bring the Blue."

"That's my girl."

The boardroom lights hum softly. Jessica sits beside Mr. Hi-Tao's motionless body. His lunch is half-eaten.

Samuel enters carrying two glasses and the bottle. He stops short.

"What the hell happened?!"

"I'm no doctor," Jessica says, "but it looks like he's dead. And shrimp was added to his lunch today."

"What? He orders the same thing every—" Samuel stops. "Someone tampered with it?"

"Yes. In fifteen keystrokes." She looks up at him, expression unreadable. "Funny how no one ever checks the health-insurance forms employees fill out. Including allergy information."

Samuel pales. "Jessica... do you know what you've done?"

"*Us?*" she echoes. "There is no *us*. Not anymore."

She lifts her phone, reading from the messages she intercepted. "'Either fall on your sword, or cut her head off with it.'"

Samuel blinks rapidly. "What are you saying?"

"I'm saying you sold me out."

Samuel swallows hard, then reaches down slowly —toward the steak knife.

Jessica smiles. "Predictable."

She draws a small pistol from her blazer—the Christmas gift she'd given Crystal years earlier—and levels it at him.

"You brought a knife to a gunfight, old man."

"You think you've won?" His voice shakes. "I told the authorities yesterday about your role in the jumper's death. They are on their way to arrest you right now. *You* chose the time and place. And no one will ever believe I'm smart enough to alter Hi-Tao's lunch order."

"Well then," Jessica says softly, "let's see who goes down harder."

She fires once—straight through his left eye. Samuel collapses, knocking over a chair as he falls, the knife still clutched in his hand.

Jessica sets the pistol on the table, trembling as the reality of what she's done descends.

The elevator bell rings.

Her breath stops.

Men spill into the hallway giving orders. Search everything. No one leaves.

Panic hits like a vise. She flees to the roof.

Night has gathered over Manhattan. She walks to the ledge, staring at the spot where the broker jumped.

For a moment, she wonders if fate intends the same end for her.

"No," she whispers. "Not like that." She turns—and freezes.

"Jessica Aguilera," Justice says as he steps forward. "I am Justice. We are here for you."

"Well, Detective Justice, cuff me or don't, but I want my phone call."

"I'm not a detective," Justice replies. "I'm here to introduce you to the Reaper of Fear."

"Great," she mutters, already looking past him. "You detectives have strange names."

Fear materializes behind Justice, voice quiet, precise. "I know your greatest fear, Jessica."

Jessica's pulse stutters.

"Twelve years ago, you said goodbye to your mother. Heart failure. She was forty-eight. Your father died at forty. That fear has lived in you ever since."

Her right arm throbs suddenly—deep, sharp pain. Jessica clutches her chest.

"It's happening now," Fear says. "A clot. Moving fast. You won't stand trial. But you also won't leave this roof alive."

Jessica gasps. "I can't die like this."

"Why not?" Fear asks.

Her legs buckle. She hits the gravel, face paling to earthly white, then to Reaper grey.

Fear's crow caws overhead and lifts Jessica's soul into the night.

Justice moves to the ledge, looking down at the street far below.

"I don't know who you were," he murmurs to the unseen broker, "or where you are now. But I hope some measure of justice reached you today."

He turns and rejoins the three Reapers.

"So, Keres," Kharon asks, "what fear did you use?"

"Cardiophobia," Keres replies.

"Ooooh, *nice*," Kara sings.

Justice nods to Keres. "Thank you for your help. Out of curiosity—what's your crow's name?"

"Phobia," Keres answers.

Justice gives a small smile. "Fitting."

Chapter 20: Sergeant Robert Michaels

Justice sits in his stone chair in the Great Chamber, the air around him pulsing faintly as he reaches forward into the strands of foresight. Visions shimmer across his consciousness—fragments of violence, judgment, the echoes of souls not yet taken. He narrows his focus, seeking the next moment where justice must be rendered.

The visions ripple, collapse.

Mercy and Lord Grim materialize before him.

Startled, Justice rises. "My Lord... my Lady... is there a reaping you require of me?"

Mercy's tone is calm but purposeful. "We need you present at a special reaping. As an observer only."

Lord Grim's dark cloak shifts like shadow caught in wind. "Find your brother Reaper War on Earth. Together, the two of you will watch over Gunnery Sergeant Robert Michaels."

The command vibrates through the chamber. Justice bows his head, and the world folds.

He appears amid the dense jungle of western Mindanao, Philippines—the humid darkness alive with insects, distant engines, and the low electrical hum of tension. Below him, a United States Marine Corps Raider unit cuts through the foliage on a covert recovery mission. Their objective: extract kidnapped missionaries held by the Sundu Mara Brigade, known to the Marines as the Mara Brigade—a ruthless militant faction whose hostages rarely leave alive.

Not knowing where else to begin, Justice calls into the shadows, "War—are you here?"

"Right behind you."

War steps out from between the trees, his war mace slung across his back. He looks Justice over with a soldier's quick appraisal. "What brings you to this lovely corner of chaos?"

"I was sent by Lord Grim and Mercy. They told me to find you, and that we are to look after Gunnery Sergeant Robert Michaels."

War raises a brow. "Michaels isn't on my list. Are you sure you heard correctly?"

"Yes." Justice folds his arms. "He isn't on mine either. I don't know why we're here."

"That makes it interesting." War's expression darkens, thoughtful. "Rare, but not unheard of. I know the Sergeant. Let me tell you what I know, and maybe the reason will reveal itself."

Justice listens.

"Michaels is part of the 2nd Marine Raider Battalion—Echo Company," War explains. "They're joined by an attached element of Air Force Pararescue. High-skill QRF. They're here to counter a Mara Brigade cell known for brutality. Hostages are shields to them—meant to stop drone strikes, nothing more."

"That explains your presence," Justice says. "But not mine. Am I here to bring justice to the militants?"

War shakes his head. "No. Their end is already coming. This is about him. The Sergeant."

Justice nods once. "Then let's find Gunnery Michaels and see why we've been called."

The jungle shudders as rotor wash sweeps overhead. A pair of choppers hover low through the treetops.

Inside the lead aircraft, Captain Weaver raises his voice over the rumble. "Alright, you all know the briefing. Once we're on the ground, it's three clicks to the target encampment. Jungle's thick—satellite couldn't give us a clean read. Stay vigilant. Intel says our hostages were spotted this afternoon, but we're treating everything as unconfirmed. This is a grab-and-go mission. Scout teams verify once we hit the ground."

"Sir!" Corporal Trejo calls. "Guns hot as needed?"

"Yes, Corporal. Confirm your targets."

"Thank you for asking this time, T," Gunnery Michaels mutters dryly.

A crackle of laughter fills the headsets.

"What're you laughing at, Motley?" Trejo shoots back. "I'm thinking I'll ask one of the missionaries to re-baptize you. After what you did with that last 'two-o'clock ten,' you're gonna need holy water, prayer, and penicillin."

"That'll teach me to let you choose first," Motley fires back.

More laughter.

The pilot cuts in. "Zero zero four five—two minutes to fast ropes."

Michaels kisses the small cross around his neck and tucks it into his uniform. "Refocus. Lock and load. Heads on swivels."

The choppers descend into the canopy. Rotors blast leaves outward as the Raiders rope down in quick succession, night-vision goggles snapping into place. Overhead, Apaches hover high, scanning the treeline with heat signatures.

The Marines form up.

"Radio check," Weaver says quietly.

Eight muted responses answer him.

"Hand signals only from here. Michaels, Trejo, Motley—you're scout team one. Move fast. We've got two hours of bird cover before the gunship has to refuel."

"Roger." Michaels signals his men forward. "NV on. Move."

Justice and War trail silently behind them, unseen, unheard.

The scout team slips through dense undergrowth, pausing only to confirm movement and count sentries. The Mara Brigade campsite materializes ahead—larger than anticipated, perimeter lit by scattered torches and dim lanterns. Hostages are identifiable in clusters.

Michaels signals and whispers, "Anyone got eyes on the three?"

"I've got the husband and wife," Motley says softly. "Thirteen hotheads on the east side. Three-man team could get in and out if we stay low and quiet."

"I saw the Pastor," Trejo adds. "They've got him in the first bunk. Twenty-one militants on the west side. We're outnumbered four to one."

"Stay cool, T," Michaels replies. "This is grab-and-go. Drones will wipe the place after extraction. They're not moving hostages tonight. Let's regroup."

They withdraw without sound.

Back with the team, Michaels briefs Captain Weaver. Weaver listens, jaw clenching.

"We split," Weaver decides. "Five with me for the double recovery. Four with Michaels for the single. Numbers favor the east, but mission is mission."

"Silencers on everything," Michaels reminds them.

Trejo asks, "If shit hits the fan, Sir?"

"Loud and deadly," Michaels answers before the captain can. "Shock and awe while we run with the hostages. Preferably alive."

Motley nudges Trejo. "Hey Romeo, keep that knife quiet this time."

"You two need couples therapy," Michaels mutters.

Payne adds, "We'd send your 'two-a.m.' friend too, but you'd turn therapy into a threesome."

Weaver snaps, "Radio silence."

Trejo and Motley exchange exaggerated winks, then both teams move out.

The jungle swallows them instantly.

Both teams fan out toward the Mara Brigade compound, shadows among shadows. Justice watches the Marines move with a precision that borders on ritual; War observes with the familiarity of someone who has walked beside warriors since the first blade was forged.

The east team reaches its target first. Ten outer guards—"hotheads," as Trejo calls them—fall silently, one by one. Weaver signals two Marines to cover the perimeter while he and two others slip into the hostel holding the husband and wife.

Three points of entry.

Three suppressed shots.

Three bodies drop.

Thirty seconds later, Weaver emerges with the two missionaries, shaken but alive.

"Take them out," he tells his four-man escort. "Stay quiet until you're a click out. Then radio for pickup."

They vanish into the trees.

Weaver turns to head toward Michaels' position, but a soft, urgent voice stops him. The rescued woman steps forward, trembling. "What about our Pastor? You have to save him."

Weaver places a hand on her shoulder. "Everyone gets out tonight. I'm heading to the second team now. Stay quiet. Follow instructions. Go."

He disappears into the darkness.

Michaels briefs him the moment he arrives. "We took down ten of the twenty-one. Eleven are still inside with the Pastor. They're alert now. Crossfire will be bad. And once they return fire, every camp within running distance will know."

Weaver nods grimly. "No one left behind. Kill them all. Let God sort them out."

The five Marines share a quiet, unanimous: "Oorah."

They breach.

Silencers whisper at first. Then the militants realize they are under attack, and the suppressed gunfire shifts to full chaos—shouts, ricochets, rounds tearing splinters from walls. Justice winces as stray rounds pass through the intangible space where he stands. War doesn't flinch.

A minute later, the Raiders spill out with Pastor Rochelle. Two Marines limp—Trejo clutching his arm, Michaels pressing a wound low on his abdomen.

Weaver moves to them. "Talk to me. Michaels—how bad?"

"Left side, through and through. No vitals. But running's gonna make it bleed faster." He steadies himself. "Get them moving. I'll catch up."

Weaver turns to Trejo. "Corporal?"

"Flesh wound. Good to go."

"Then we go loud," Weaver decides. "Motley—stay with Michaels. Everyone else, run with the Pastor. Move!"

The jungle detonates around them. Militants pour from neighboring camps in a chaotic flood of gunfire. Rounds snap through branches, carving lines of fire in the night.

The main group runs hard, covering the Pastor as best they can. The two-man team—Michaels and Motley—lags behind, trading accurate bursts for the others' safety.

Justice and War watch from just behind the veil.

"Mortals never cease to surprise me," Justice murmurs. Michaels' determination pulses like a beacon —bright, defiant, human.

War's voice is low. "This is the part where purpose starts revealing itself."

A second encampment joins the fight. Rounds hiss past Michaels' helmet. Motley ducks, spins, fires a controlled burst. Then a round slams into his shoulder, knocking him back into a half-spin.

"Michaels—I'm—!"

His warning cuts off as he sees the grenade.

It arcs in slow motion—at least to Justice's eyes— falling through a shaft of faint moonlight and landing at Motley's feet.

Before Motley can curse, run, or breathe, Michaels lunges.

He hits Motley hard, shoving him backward, and throws himself onto the grenade.

The explosion lifts Michaels off the ground.

Motley watches, horrified, as shrapnel tears into the Gunnery Sergeant, the force flinging him upward and dropping him hard onto the jungle floor.

"NO! NO NO NO!" Motley crawls toward him, dragging his wounded arm, mud and leaves streaking his uniform. He rolls Michaels over, and the world seems to halt as he stares into the glassy, unblinking eyes of a man already gone.

Motley makes a sound—somewhere between a sob and a curse—and presses his forehead to Michaels' chest.

The firefight still rages, but he doesn't hear it.

Justice stands frozen. "Is this the moment we were meant to witness?"

War nods once. "Wait."

Something shifts.

The jungle quiets—not in sound, but in weight. A familiar pressure settles over the clearing.

Above the canopy, a new sound rises—not mechanical, not human. A resonant chord, richer and deeper than thunder.

Justice looks up.

A seam opens in the clouds, spilling brilliance onto the battlefield. The air glows; smoke softens; even the trees seem to bow.

A legion of Heaven's Warrior Angels descends in perfect formation, wings spread in shimmering arcs of light. At their center is **Angel Zadkiel**, moving with a grace that silences the world.

Michaels' body lies crumpled below, but Zadkiel kneels beside him with reverence, gathering the Marine's soul—now luminous, peaceful, whole—into his arms.

Justice bows his head.

War whispers, "This is as close to Heaven as Reapers ever come."

The Angels rise as one, lifting Michaels' soul into the widening rift of light. Their voices join in an otherworldly hymn that vibrates through the ground, through Justice, through everything.

Below, Motley and Payne lift Michaels' body and start toward the extraction zone.

Overhead, the distant helicopter grows louder.

The hymn fades.

The clouds close.

Darkness returns.

The remaining Marines break through the final stretch of jungle, Pastor Rochelle between them as they fire backward into the darkness. The gunship overhead unleashes a controlled burst meant to scatter the militants, not annihilate them—yet even that distant roar shakes leaves from branches.

Captain Weaver reaches the clearing first, guiding the Pastor toward the waiting helicopter. The moment the Pastor's feet are on the skid, Weaver pivots to look for the others.

Payne and Motley appear next—Motley stumbling, cradling his injured shoulder with one hand, supporting Michaels' lifeless body with the other. The weight drags him to one knee before Payne hauls him upright again.

Weaver rushes to help them. "Get him in! Move, move!"

Motley snarls through gritted teeth, "Don't—don't drop him—"

"No one's dropping him," Weaver says, voice iron. Together the three Marines lift Michaels' body into the bird. Motley climbs in after him, collapsing beside his fallen friend, blood soaking through his sleeve.

"Where's the rest?" the pilot yells.

"Everyone's here!" Weaver shouts back. "Go!"

148

The helicopter lifts, rotors beating the humid air into submission. The jungle drops away beneath them as tracer rounds streak upward but fall short.

Inside the aircraft, Pastor Rochelle grips the bench, whispering prayers. Payne sits opposite Motley, his face hard, his eyes wet. Weaver crouches beside Michaels' body, one hand resting briefly on the fallen Marine's shoulder.

Motley stares at Michaels' still form, jaw clenched. "He saved my life," he whispers. "He… he didn't even think. Just—" He swallows. "Just did it."

Weaver nods, voice low. "That's who he was."

The pilot calls back, "Two minutes to ghost ship coverage!"

No one responds. The cabin is too full of grief, adrenaline, and the heaviness that follows bravery no one wanted to witness.

Justice and War stand in the clearing long after the helicopter fades from sight, long after the gunfire dies, long after the militants scatter in confusion. The jungle slowly returns to itself—the insects resume their drone, leaves settle, smoke thins.

Justice lets out a breath. "War… that was unlike any mortal death I've seen."

War watches the canopy where Heaven's rift once glowed. "Some souls earn moments like that. Zadkiel himself doesn't descend often. When he does, it's for a reason."

Justice's gaze follows where the Angels rose. "You said this was as close as we come to Heaven."

"And it is." War turns to him. "We serve Lord Grim. Our place is between worlds—not in the one above."

Justice bows his head. "Then Michaels was truly honored."

"He was." War adjusts the war mace he never uses —a gesture more habit than need. "He'll be laid to rest in the national cemetery of his homeland. Full honors. Flag-draped casket. Twenty-one rifle salute. Missing man flyover. Purple Heart—his third. And the Medal of Honor, posthumously."

Justice closes his eyes briefly. "A fitting remembrance."

War gives a small nod. "This will be one for the history books, Justice. Mortals will speak his name for generations."

He steps back into the deeper shadow between two broad trees, the jungle swallowing him without sound. "I've got work elsewhere. Until we meet again."

Justice watches him vanish, the last echoes of the battle fading into the rustling leaves. The jungle breathes, life moving on, unaware of the celestial honor it has briefly hosted.

He stands alone now, the air still tinged with the afterglow of Heaven's passage, and whispers, "Amen."

The light around him bends—and he is gone.

Chapter 21: What I am here for

Justice looks over at the chair beside him, where the Reaper of Vengeance sits in meditation, still as stone.

"Vengeance, how would you like to come with me on a reaping?" Justice asks.

Vengeance doesn't open his eyes. "I've heard you've been dragging other Reapers into your assignments. Why invite me?"

"This one's a hot-shot defense lawyer," Justice says, leaning back with a half-smile. "The kind who debates, denies, deflects—and likes to hear himself talk. I thought you might enjoy a little fun."

Vengeance finally opens one eye, studying him. "You allow them to argue with you?"

"No. But tag-teaming an attorney sounded entertaining."

Vengeance considers this for a moment. "Reaping a scumbag attorney…" He gives a slow, appreciative nod. "Yes. That does sound fun. Fill me in while we travel."

Outside the Grand City Courthouse, tension hangs so thick it could be carved. For weeks, reporters from across the country have camped on the courthouse steps waiting for the verdict in the trial of Ivan Romananski—a case inflated by scandal, money, a dead supermodel, Russian mob ties, and a legal team with a reputation for winning the unwinnable.

Romananski, now a respected importer of Northern European commercial goods, once served in the Soviet Army in the 1980s. During that time, he forged ties with the Russian mob—ties that became partnerships and then friendships. When he expanded into the American market, he discovered Grand City's fast-paced glamour. At one of the many galas (no one remembers which), he met American supermodel Sandra Siri. Their courtship unfolded under the public eye, photos of them at family gatherings and religious events plastered across magazines.

They married, proudly leaning into their Jewish heritage—but as the years passed, the coverage faded. Until Sandra died, and Romananski became the lead suspect.

Judge Allen Bona dismissed key evidence due to improper handling. The public was outraged.

The courthouse doors open. The crowd surges as District Attorney Scott Scharton steps outside with his team.

"It was Judge Bona's unfortunate decision to deem our key evidence inadmissible," he says tightly. "While we disagree, we will not seek a retrial, due to the financial strain on the city and the continued suffering of Ms. Siri's family. Thank you."

Reporters erupt with questions as he leaves.

Then the defense team emerges. Attorney James Luther steps forward, flashing his million-dollar smile.

"Yes, BJ?" he calls to a reporter in the back.

"What really happened—and I love the new suit," BJ says.

"Sloppy police work," Luther replies smoothly. "Next question. Steve?"

"Is it true this was the largest payout for your team?"

Luther doesn't miss a beat. "You get what you pay for."

Behind him, Sandra Siri's family exits the courthouse. Her younger sister Barbara snaps when a reporter presses her about the verdict.

"How do I feel? It's complete bullshit! Everyone knows Ivan killed my sister. And no fancy lawyer is going to save him from what's coming."

Thirty miles outside of town, a mid-size sedan pulls into the parking lot of a small diner. Lieutenant Lane Roars checks his watch, puts on a baseball cap, and scans the almost-empty lot. Even off duty—and currently suspended—he thinks like a cop.

Inside, the diner is nearly deserted. The waitress rolls silverware at the counter.

"Sit anywhere!" she calls.

Lane chooses a corner booth facing the door but away from the windows. He notices a TV playing news coverage of the Romananski trial. He stares a second too long.

"You okay, hon? Looks like you've seen a ghost," the waitress says, eyeing him.

Lane forces a blink. "Just tired. Coffee, black."

"You got it," she says. Her nametag reads *Gert*.

Lane's mind returns to the headline on TV. How did I get into this? I'm a good cop… so why did I 'lose' that shovel?

He gets up to use the restroom. When he returns, a young man is sitting in his booth.

"What the hell are you doing?" Lane snaps.

"No worries," the young man says casually. "I ordered my own coffee. Yours is right there. And I paid for both."

Lane opens his mouth to object, but the young man cuts him off.

"Sit. You can call me Timmy."

Lane reluctantly sits. "I shouldn't be seen with you."

Timmy laughs. "Look around. The place is empty. And if you tip Gert a hundred bucks, I promise she won't remember you were here."

"Not sure I can afford that," Lane mutters.

"Cheer up. I'm here to end all your troubles." Timmy nudges a large envelope across the table. "This is just the first visit. You'll be hearing from us again."

Timmy stands and walks out. Lane slips the envelope under the table, opens it, and sees stacks of crisp hundred-dollar bills.

He looks up—but Timmy is gone. Only the bell on the diner door gives any sign he was real.

Lane bolts, leaving without tipping Gert.

Meanwhile, Defense Attorney James Luther storms into his corner office, calling to his secretary, "Hold all my calls!"

He slams the door—then freezes.

Someone is sitting in the visitor's chair.

Luther frowns. "Can I help you?" He sets down his briefcase and reaches for his phone. "I don't have any appointments, and I don't know how you got past my—"

"Don't blame Bobbie," the stranger says. "This appointment is off the books."

Luther's gaze drops to the man's T-shirt. *Blue Oyster Cult.* "You're definitely not a lawyer. If you need one, check the fourth floor. I'm not taking new clients. So please leave."

The man smiles faintly. "Don't Fear the Reaper. Their biggest charting U.S. hit. Billboard Hot 100, 20 weeks. Peaked at number twelve in November '76."

"How fascinating," Luther deadpans. "Tell it to someone who cares. I have work to—"

"The funny part?" the man interrupts. "They weren't wrong. But it's not us Reapers humans should fear—it's what comes after."

Luther stops. "Reapers? Seriously?"

A new voice speaks behind him. "Luther, you should be afraid."

Justice sits in his desk chair.

Luther spins around, rattled. "If you two are 'Reapers'... what do you reap?"

"I am the Reaper of Justice," Justice says steadily. "This is Vengeance. And we're here because you're guilty. We've come to collect."

"Guilty of what? Who are you to judge me?"

Justice crouches beside him. "Let's start small. Remember *Swain vs. Splits Corporation*? You bankrupted a small business. Mrs. Swain couldn't afford the surgery she needed. She ended up paralyzed."

Luther collapses to the floor—paralyzed from the waist down.

Justice continues. "And Ms. Heart? Kidnapped and tortured by Mr. Keim. Over a thousand razor cuts. You turned her suffering into a legal strategy. Got your client moved to a luxury psychiatric facility. Tennis by day, poker by night."

A folder materializes. Justice drops photos of Ms. Heart onto Luther's chest—each photo producing a fresh cut on Luther's skin.

Luther screams.

"Stop! Please! I didn't *kill* them!"

Justice tilts his head. "Sandra Siri? Buried alive. Do you think she begged? Do you think she pleaded? You'll have the same number of breaths she had."

Luther gasps. "Vengeance is mine, saith the Lord —Deuteronomy—32:35—You can't—"

Vengeance steps forward, laughing softly.

"Oh, Luther. You can even deceive yourself. But *that* is what I am here for."

Luther takes his final breath. His body turns grey. A raven swoops in, then disappears.

As Justice and Vengeance leave:

1. Gert still doesn't get her tip.

2. She makes an anonymous call to police.

3. A not-so-good cop gets arrested.

Remember: always tip your waitress.

Chapter 22: The Gambler

Back in the chamber, Justice sits with his eyes closed, searching the earthly world with his gift of foresight. He is so deep in his own mind that he doesn't hear Lady Mercy enter.

Standing in front of him, Mercy says, "The gift of foresight is granted to the Reaper of Justice to seek out those who must be held accountable for their actions—and to protect the greater good. It is not an ability to spy on your daughter."

Justice's eyes open. He looks up at her sheepishly. "My apologies."

"Very well," Mercy replies, her tone softening. "Tell me about your daughter."

Slightly shocked that she knows, Justice exhales and starts to share. "Her name is Alyssa. She's twenty-five now. She graduated from college with a degree in accounting—a very smart girl, all from her mother's side. I hoped she'd go back for her CPA and keep moving forward in that field. But with her mother's and my death, I'm afraid she's a little lost right now. She's financially okay because of the trust funds we set up for her. But with money comes... certain issues."

"Since the creation of money, it has been the root of many earthly evils," Mercy says. "What issue is Alyssa facing that makes you feel compelled to watch over her daily?"

"Love leeches."

Mercy tilts her head. "I'm not familiar with that term. What are 'love leeches'?"

"Sorry, Lady Mercy. There are still a lot of earthly phrases I like to use." Justice smiles faintly. "Love leeches are people—friends, boyfriends—who attach themselves to someone with money. In Alyssa's case, there's a young man who keeps saying things like, 'If you love me, you'll buy me this,' or 'We should go on a trip.' He's clever about finding ways to get her to spend her money on him.

"And she's vulnerable right now. She's still grieving her mother—and me. The feeling of being loved by anyone seems better than the feeling of being loved by no one."

"Heartbreaking," Mercy says. "To see one's only child go through something like that would be painful for any parent. But this problem means nothing beyond the earthly realm."

Justice drops his gaze.

"I suggest you leave her alone for six months and see how she grows," Mercy continues gently. "You might be surprised by the daughter you have already raised. In the meantime, put your gift back to its proper use before Lord Grim decides to take it away."

"Yes, of course, my Lady." Justice straightens slightly. "Now that you mention it, there is a young man who's come into my visions a few times. I believe his situation could use your special care. Do you have time to assist me?"

"Yes," Mercy says. "How can I help?"

"I'm hoping to give this young man, Wendell, some mercy—so he can get back on his feet. He's made poor choices with good intentions. Wendell is a second-rate gambler, and his wife and son may soon suffer for his inability to stop."

"This sounds interesting," Mercy replies, "but you and Wendell do not need *my* help. My sister, Lady Luck, is better suited to this situation."

"A sister?" Justice blinks. "Lady Luck is real—and your sister?"

"Of course she's real," Mercy says with a wry look. "But the relationship is... complicated. I use the word 'sister' loosely so your mind has something to latch onto."

"Would you be able to introduce us?"

"I am happy to facilitate the meeting," Mercy says, "but Lady Luck cannot enter the chamber. The introduction will take place at Janing's Pub."

"You really don't miss much, do you?"

"Correct," Mercy says. "I have been doing this longer than all of you combined. We should go, before Lord Grim *does* take that looking glass of yours."

The door creaks as Justice steps into Janing's Pub. A sliver of twilight cuts across the room before the door closes behind him. Justice scans the mostly empty space and makes his way to the bar.

"Hello, Tracy," he says. "Good to see you again."

"Welcome back, Drake," Tracy replies. "The usual?"

"Yes, that would be great."

"Coming right up. I'll bring it to you. Usual table, right? Anyone joining you?"

"Yes," Justice says, "but I'm not sure when she'll arrive. I thought I'd enjoy a drink first."

"Sounds good. As long as you're drinking, it's no business of mine what company you keep." Tracy shrugs. "I just hope she's nothing like that last group you were in here with. No offense, but they were a little weird."

"Fair enough," Justice says with a small smile. "I think this one will be okay."

Tracy leaves him with his first shot of Johnny Walker Blue. Over the next hour, the bar fills in. Justice has two more drinks and settles into people-watching as he waits. He wonders if Mercy will appear with Lady Luck, or if he'll just somehow *know*.

As the thought leaves his mind, the bar door swings open and a gust of night air rushes in. Every man in the place looks up.

There she is.

Lady Luck.

Before she even crosses the room, two men step in front of her, offering to buy her a drink.

"Thank you, boys, but I'm good," she says with a wink. "I'm meeting a friend."

She glides toward Justice's table. When she reaches it, she smiles down at him. For a moment, he simply stares.

"Well?" she asks. "Are you going to ask me to sit, or what?"

Justice clears his throat. "Uhm… yes. Please—have a seat. Can I get you a drink?"

"Thank you," Lady Luck says. "I'll have whatever you're having."

"Tracy? Two more, please!" Justice calls over the din.

"Sure thing, coming right up!" Tracy answers.

He brings over two more shots of Johnny Walker Blue and sets them down. Justice looks up to thank him and is caught off guard by the wide grin on Tracy's face.

"Thank you, Tracy," Justice says slowly. "Are you all right?"

"I couldn't be better!" Tracy announces, a little too loudly. "This round's on the house."

"Oh, really?" Justice asks. "Are you sure?"

"Yes!" Tracy laughs. "Just got word the bar passed all its health inspections, and my liquor license is renewed for five more years. This is my lucky day."

He heads back to the bar, humming.

Justice turns back to Lady Luck with a suspicious look. "Is that your doing?"

"What can I say?" she replies, lifting her glass. "I ooze good things—for everyone nearby. Now, what do you have in mind for me?"

"I need a down-and-out gambler, Wendell Short, to catch a break," Justice says. "He's buried his wife and son in debt, and I'm hoping a win might help him get straight and get out."

"So," Lady Luck says, "what are you thinking? Lottery ticket?"

"No. Lottery winners are usually broke again within three years. Probably faster for a gambler. For people like him, it's not the money—it's the dopamine rush. The winning is the addiction."

"Agreed," she says. "So we go with poker. I can control it more easily. You wouldn't believe the prayers sent up to the 'poker gods' during a tournament. Sadly, most of those get rerouted to me."

Justice chuckles.

"Let's use the L.A. Poker Classic," she continues. "First prize is a little over three hundred thousand. Four days of play, about six hundred forty-five entries. Less than a week's work."

"If I remember right from my poker days, that's a fifteen-hundred-dollar buy-in," Justice says. "He doesn't have that."

"He can satellite in for a hundred fifty," Lady Luck says.

"If he satellites in, he'll probably sell the entry—or gamble it away before he even gets there," Justice counters.

"True," she concedes. "So I'll arrange a 'lucky draw' on some crappy online game he plays—a special clause that only he can redeem. That way, he gets the seat and keeps it."

"Sounds solid," Justice says. "Although after all the laptop controversies last year at the World Series of Poker—cheating signals, hidden devices—giving him nonstop luck might make the stats go wild."

"Well, I'm a little rusty," Lady Luck says with a mischievous smile, "but maybe it's my turn to have a little fun. Besides, you know the old proverb: 'Lucky at cards, unlucky in love.'"

"Are *you* unlucky in love?" Justice asks.

"Lady Love is another sister you've yet to meet," she replies.

"What?" Justice groans. "More sisters? I'm not sure we have time for all this. We should head to Los Angeles—and make sure Wendell gets there too."

In a small apartment, Carla finishes cleaning up dinner while her son Eric plays in the next room. A knock at the door startles her. Before she reaches it, the knob turns and Wendell steps inside.

"What are you doing here?" Carla snaps. "I'm not sure I'm over you gambling our house away."

"Fair enough," Wendell says. "But I'm still your husband—and Eric's father." He sighs. "I miss you guys. I haven't seen you in a while."

"I miss my *husband* too," Carla replies. "And yes, Eric misses his *father*. So—did you get a job?"

"No," Wendell says, brightening, "but I've got something even better. I won an entry into the L.A. Poker Classic. First place is three hundred thousand dollars. Do you know what that means? We'd be set for life!"

Carla rolls her eyes. "Wendell, that's not a job. It's another dead end. Or a continuation of this whole nightmare. Why don't you sell the entry and catch up some of your—*our*—debts? I love you, but I have to look out for Eric's future. Besides, even if you do win, every casino around here has banned you since you 'shot that angel.'"

With a little chuckle, Wendell corrects, "It's called 'angle shooting,' and it was never proven." He waves that away. "Look, I was hoping you'd be excited—see that I'm trying to fix this. I know I can do this. When I win, I'll make a better life for us. I love you, Carla. And I love Eric."

He gives her one more hopeful look, then leaves the apartment.

The L.A. sun blazes as the motley mix of hopefuls, railbirds, and exhausted survivors file into the Commerce Casino for the final day of the L.A. Poker Classic. After three long days, the field has narrowed to just two players.

Amazingly, neither is a professional. Neither has ever cashed in a major tournament.

It's a Cinderella story for both.

"Welcome back, folks," the local commentator says. "We're down to Cheryl Johnson from Warren, Pennsylvania, and Wendell Short from Durham, North Carolina. Their chip stacks are nearly even—only two big blinds separating them. With blinds this high, it will take just one big hand to decide it all."

169

(Throughout the tournament, Lady Luck has been "playing" as Cheryl and has been oozing luck Wendell's way—nudging cards, timing, and decisions—until now, when she and Wendell face each other heads-up.)

"The blinds are four hundred thousand and eight hundred thousand," the commentator continues, "with an eight hundred thousand big blind ante. At this level, the blinds force big pots—and often all-in decisions."

Cheryl is dealt the two of clubs and the seven of diamonds in the big blind.
Wendell, in the small blind, looks down at the ace and king of clubs. He limps in, just calling the big blind.

"Pre-flop advantage: roughly sixty-eight percent to thirty percent in Wendell's favor," the commentator notes. "Interesting choice to just limp. Let's see what Cheryl does."

Cheryl decides to take advantage of his passivity and raises to 1.4 million.

Wendell just calls, wanting to see a flop in case she's holding a pocket pair.

The flop comes:

Four of clubs.

Six of clubs.

Five of clubs.

"Wow," the commentator says. "What an incredible flop for Wendell. He flops the ace-high flush. The odds swing hard in his favor—ninety-five and a half percent to four and a half."

Both players check.

"Slow play from both," the commentator says. "Wendell is trapping. Cheryl is hoping to catch up."

The turn is the three of diamonds.

"A brutal card for Cheryl," the commentator continues. "It gives her an open-ended straight draw from seven down to the deuce—but it does nothing against the ace-high flush Wendell already has. Her odds drop to just over two percent. His climb to over ninety-seven."

Wendell leads out with a sizable bet—six million, leaving himself only two million behind.

"Great sizing," the commentator says. "Not shoving all in, but putting real pressure on. To Cheryl, this could look like a flush *draw* instead of a made hand."

Cheryl studies the board, then pushes her towers of chips forward.

"All in," she says.

Wendell tilts his head, looks back at his cards, and then breaks into a grin.

171

"I call."

The tournament director instructs them both to table their cards. The dealer flips them face up, revealing Wendell's ace-high flush—and Cheryl's straight with a redraw to a straight flush.

"She needs exactly one card," the commentator says. "The three of clubs. One out in the deck."

Cheryl sits perfectly still, eyes never leaving Wendell. Wendell strides along the rail, slapping high fives with spectators who have already written Cheryl off.

"Dealer, the river card, please," the tournament director says.

The burn card is placed aside. The river card slides onto the felt. The dealer hooks it with a fingernail and slowly turns it over.

The three of clubs.

The room gasps.

Cheryl doesn't move; her gaze remains on Wendell as the dealer pushes the pot and arranges the winning straight flush to her.

Wendell stops mid-stride, wide-eyed and confused, and rushes back to the table.

After a quick count, the tournament director steps forward with the trophy and the oversized first-place check. "Ladies and gentlemen, your L.A. Poker Classic champion—Cheryl Johnson—with total winnings of three hundred twenty-three thousand, eight hundred seventy-six dollars!"

Cheryl shakes Wendell's hand. "Congratulations, Wendell. You played very well. I hope you get home safely—and I hope your winnings help you and your family."

She turns to the crowd. "Commerce Casino has been a wonderful host. I'd like to ask that all my winnings be donated to the Women's Breast Cancer Research Center. Thank you."

The crowd rises to a standing ovation. Cheryl sets the trophy beside the winning hand and walks away.

Wendell watches her go, then collects his second-place payout and the few belongings from his room. He catches the first flight home to North Carolina.

He arrives back at the apartment at 2:30 a.m., quietly sets his bag and winnings by the door, and tiptoes to the bedroom. Carla is asleep.

"Carla," he whispers. "Carla, I'm home."

She stirs. "What time is it?"

"Two-thirty," Wendell says. "I'm sorry. But I've got some great news—"

"Your great news can wait until I've had coffee," Carla mumbles. "Go sleep on the sofa. When it's a decent hour, you can come back—with my coffee—and tell me all about it."

Wendell smiles despite himself. "Okay. I'm exhausted anyway. Not sure I'll sleep, but… okay."

As he closes the door, he hears her murmur, "Don't forget—two sugars."

He heads to the sofa and lies awake, floating on the thought that everything is about to change. When early light begins to creep into the living room, he decides to walk to the coffee shop two blocks away. He wants to surprise Carla with a "fancy" coffee and a muffin for Eric.

He grabs a hundred-dollar bill and heads out, leaving his wallet on the side table without realizing it.

Feeling buoyant, Wendell orders two coffees and a muffin. When he pays, he leaves a fifty-dollar tip, and that makes him feel even better. He pictures Carla's face when he hands her the coffee and the cash. He imagines Eric's delight at the muffin.

Then, suddenly, a strange warmth floods his body. The all-too-familiar metallic taste of blood fills his mouth.

He barely has time to set the coffees and muffin down and press a tissue to his nose before he collapses.

Wendell is transported from the coffee shop unconscious, by ambulance, to the nearest hospital. With no identification on him, he's admitted as a John Doe. The ER team works feverishly to stabilize him.

Outside the room, Justice stands with Lady Luck and Lady Mercy.

They listen as the crisis inside finally begins to calm, leaving only one nurse with Wendell. Justice turns to the two Eternals.

"He's been diagnosed with stage four leukemia," Justice says quietly. "What are our options now?"

"How strange," Lady Luck muses. "This kind of cancer is like gambling—it's in his blood and it never really goes away. And everyone's luck runs out at some point. The World Series of Poker is starting in Las Vegas soon, and… well, you know." She gives Justice a little wink. "Bye for now, Justice. I loved working with you. Stay lucky."

She disappears.

Justice looks to Mercy. "This really did not go as planned. Lady Mercy, could you help?"

"Are you asking me to have mercy on him?" she asks. "Do you not want him to live, no matter how long —or short—that might be?"

"A merciful death would be better," Justice says. "Better than all his hard work being swallowed by endless hospital bills—and leaving his family even more shattered."

Mercy studies him for a long moment, then nods once. "Mercy is granted. You may show him mercy."

She, too, takes her leave.

Justice looks one last time at Wendell, pale and still on the hospital bed. A caw echoes softly. Devon glides in, circles once, and vanishes again—taking Wendell's soul with him.

Chapter 23: Earth

"No. No, and absolutely not," Justice says to himself as he scrolls through the list of evil humans as if browsing a dating app. Seated in the Great Chamber, Justice continues to use his foresight, searching for the next soul to reap. With time, he has grown more attuned to how the ability works. Following the advice of Lady Mercy, he has avoided checking in on his daughter for quite some time now.

With his eyes still closed, Justice senses that someone is watching him. He focuses on the feeling, keeping his eyes shut, and realizes he knows exactly who is there.

"Hello, Lady Mercy. What brings you here? And no—I have not checked on Alyssa for a while."

Lady Mercy gives Justice a warm smile. "I am very glad to hear that."

"I may be stubborn," Justice says, "but I do listen. You advised six months, and I am trying to honor that. Time is difficult to track in this realm. Can you tell me when I'll be able to check on her?"

"You are stubborn, yes," Lady Mercy replies, "but you are also wise. You will know when the time is right.

It is good to see you finally understanding that. Now—back to business. Who are you considering?"

Justice considers several individuals revealed through foresight before answering. "On multiple occasions, I've seen an Autobahn driver who drives too slowly while texting. She has no idea how many lives she may take one day."

"Interesting," Lady Mercy says, "but you should be thinking bigger."

"All right. There's a doctor who has made several misdiagnoses, leading to one death and leaving others far worse than if it had been handled correctly the first time."

"Horrible," she agrees, "but still—think bigger."

Justice exhales. "A television evangelist. He's making millions while abusing people in the name of God. He's dragging countless others down with him."

"TV evangelists are not your concern," Lady Mercy says. "That matter will be handled soon enough."

Justice frowns. "If none of these are sufficient, should I be looking on a global level?"

"Global," Lady Mercy says, smiling. "Yes. That is exactly the right scale."

As she fades, Justice closes his eyes and extends his foresight outward. Moments pass before he senses another presence.

"Lady Mercy, are you still—" Justice stops short as he opens his eyes.

Before him stands a seventeen-foot-tall, humanlike figure, resembling an ancient tree. Vines and leaves drape its massive form. The face appears hardened by time, deep grooves etched into bark-like skin, moss tangled thickly where a beard would be.

Unsure what else to do, Justice speaks. "Hello. I am the Reaper Justice. And your name is?"

The voice that answers is deep and resonant. "I am Earth."

Justice blinks. "Mother Earth? I imagined you differently—beautiful, gentle. What happened to you? Why are you here, and what do you want from me?"

"I was beautiful when God Almighty made me, as written in Genesis," Earth replies. "Humanity reshaped me through disregard and misuse. Hiroshima. Three Mile Island. Chernobyl. The melting of Antarctica."

Justice swallows. "How can I help? Who must be dealt with? Why come to me now?"

"My name is Samyaza," Earth says. "You are needed because you work like a scalpel. I, by contrast, work like a scythe."

Justice stiffens. "Careful. That symbol belongs to Lord Grim."

"I have worked alongside Lord Grim before," Earth says calmly. "During the Great Flood."

"Yes," Justice says. "Lord Grim has spoken of that. I believed those days were long past."

"They never ended. Earthquakes, hurricanes, tsunamis—those are my doing. But they take too much."

"Then tell me what you want."

"While Lord Grim deliberated over the appointment of the new Justice Reaper, I did what I had to do. I released my fury, and it changed me. I want you to reap the CEO of the Grilkar Corporation. Under his leadership, the damage will continue, regardless of warnings or reports. A lightning strike would end him— but his replacement would repeat the same mistakes. What is needed is fear. A lesson."

"Then let us proceed," Justice says. "But you must return to what God intended you to be."

Earth studies him. "You say that as though you still walk among the living."

"I do," Justice replies. "On occasion. There is someone there I still watch over."

"Pocket Change" is docked at Marina do Funchal, Portugal. The crew of sixteen stands at attention as the President of Grilkar Corporation—along with the owner of the ten-million-dollar yacht—passes them without so much as a glance, his attention fixed on his phone.

Once past the crew, Richard McDonald turns to his public relations manager, Helena Clarke.

"How long until Congressman Goldman arrives?"

"His flight has landed. His limo will be here in thirty minutes," Helena replies, clipped and efficient.

"Good. I want to meet with the captain and review the itinerary. Dinner in port, then crew shift change. The night crew boards after dark."

"That's correct, sir. The night crew was hand-picked by me. Party favors will arrive with them."

"Tonight is critical," Richard says. "We need the Congressman's backing—whether he agrees willingly or not. Blackmail worked with the Senator. This one may be more resistant."

"Understood," Helena says. "Lewis has arrived. Shall I send him in?"

"Yes. Thank you, Helena."

She exits the reception room and waves Lewis Drey—the current CEO of Grilkar Corporation—inside.

"Everything set?" Lewis asks.

"All aces," Richard replies.

"However this plays out tonight," Lewis says, lowering his voice, "Helena gets added to our CIA list."

"Agreed," Richard says. "She knows too much. If things go sideways, she takes the fall for the escorts and the cocaine. If it goes perfectly, she still has to go—she's the connective tissue."

"That's how we stay clean," Lewis says, glancing toward the dock. "There's the Congressman's limo. Let's begin."

They rise to greet him.

"Congressman Goldman," Richard says smoothly, "welcome to Portugal—and to what is now your private yacht. May we call you Robert?"

"Please—Bob," the Congressman says with a smile. "By the end of the weekend, I'm sure we'll be on a first-name basis."

Evening gives way to night. Dinner is served, cleared, and forgotten. The service crew disembarks, leaving only security, the bartender, the captain, and Helena aboard. From the deck, Helena watches the van carrying the dinner crew pull away. She sends several text messages, then heads toward the dock as a limo pulls up.

The driver steps out. Helena passes him a thick envelope of cash. The rear door opens, and six elegantly dressed women step onto the dock and make their way aboard the yacht. Helena nods once to the driver and returns on board. As soon as she does, departure protocols begin, and the yacht slips free of the marina.

Once underway, Helena retreats to her suite at the opposite end of the yacht from the entertainment room. The remaining crew has been instructed to stay clear of the area unless directly assigned. As the yacht reaches the open waters of the North Atlantic, the party escalates rapidly.

When the women exit the entertainment room to retrieve more powder, Justice chooses his moment.

"Gentlemen," he says calmly, materializing before them, "while your entertainment replenishes supplies, allow me to introduce myself. I am the Reaper of Justice. Tonight, I will explain which of your crimes against humanity—and the Earth—you are being punished for."

"H E L E N A!" Richard shouts. "Get in here now —and bring security!"

Justice does not react. "Deforestation across the globe has altered water systems beyond recovery. Pesticides have destroyed ecosystems and raised cancer rates in the regions you exploit. You clear land to grow soy for livestock, then bribe officials to block sustainable competitors. These choices earned you billions."

The Congressman rises. "I have nothing to do with their corporate decisions. You should let me go. I could be useful to you."

Justice looks at him with thinly veiled disdain. "Do I appear to need your help? You're buried in insider trading and kickbacks. They didn't coerce you—you volunteered."

All three men shout for security, staring at the doorway.

Justice chuckles softly. "They won't be coming. Your security team—most of whom committed their own atrocities—are currently floating in the ocean. As for Helena, the bartender, and your guests, they've already departed. Safely. In the last lifeboat."

Lewis pales. "Helena wouldn't leave us."

"She left the moment I explained what you planned for her—and what happened to her predecessor," Justice replies. "Fear has a way of clarifying loyalty."

He pauses.

"A typhoon is forming. It will tear this yacht in half."

"That's impossible," the Congressman snaps. "Storms like that are tracked days in advance. Where's the captain?"

"You're correct," Justice says evenly. "They usually are. But I have friends—one in particular. As for your captain, he's chosen to sleep through this. His last indulgence."

Justice steps back. "Unlike you, he will die calm."

Justice vanishes.

The men rush to the windows as lightning fractures the sky. Waves rise—massive, violent, relentless—towering nearly one hundred feet above the four-story yacht. In moments, the sea swallows the vessel whole. The storm is brutal and brief. The yacht is torn apart, scattered across the ocean floor.

Then, as suddenly as it began, the typhoon dissipates—traveling no more than a mile before vanishing entirely, as if someone simply switched it off.

Justice returns to the Great Chamber, where Earth waits for him. He takes his seat as Earth approaches.

"I have come to this Chamber only once before," Earth says. "It is not my realm. But I came then to ask for your help—and now I come to thank you. I feel at peace returning to my natural state, knowing that you will watch over justice, not only for humankind, but for the world they inhabit as well."

Justice inclines his head. "That responsibility was never meant to be ignored."

"Thank you, my friend," Earth says.

As the final words leave her lips, Earth's form begins to change. The scars fade. The bark smooths. The vines retreat. In their place stands the natural beauty God originally created. With a final, grateful look, Earth disappears from the Chamber.

Justice remains alone, seated in silence, the weight of the world once more balanced—if only for a time.

Chapter 24: Love Lesson

"Not that this isn't my kind of place," Kara says as she slides into the booth at Janings Pub, "but why do we *always* meet here when we're in the earthly realm?"

Drake doesn't look up from spinning his empty glass. "Proverbs 31:6: 'Give alcohol to those who are perishing and wine to those who are in bitter distress.'"

Kara's eyes go wide. "Ohhh, I didn't know the Bible was so interesting. Honestly, it wasn't exactly on my 'must read' list when I was alive." She giggles. "Actually, I don't think I *had* a must-read list."

"Really? You, not a big reader? Who would've guessed?"

Kara gasps dramatically. "Oh, that's rude. *That's* rude. Enough chit-chat. Why did you call this meeting, pretty please?" She props her elbows on the table and rests her chin on her hands like she's settling in for a gossip session.

Drake exhales and sets the glass down. "Not sure I've ever told you, but... I have a daughter. Alyssa. She's twenty-five. She has a degree in accounting—very smart girl, all from her mother's side. But after Donna passed and then me, she seems a little lost. I had hoped she'd return to school, get her CPA, keep moving forward.

She's financially stable thanks to the trust funds we set up, but with money comes... problems."

Kara goes still, eyes huge and soft. "Ugh. Boring. *Really?* No weird sexual habits? No binge-drinking? Nothing fun?"

"Watch your mouth. She's my daughter."

Kara shrugs. "Aren't we all someone's daughter? Anyway, you probably invited the wrong Reaper to drink with you. But I *do* like this Johnnie Walker Blue you keep buying, so I'll stay. Now—give me something juicy. Tattoos, maybe? Did she get a tattoo? Did I ever tell you about my Lady Valkyrie tattoo?"

Rolling his eyes, Drake groans. "Yes. Too many times. And yes—her 'love leech' boyfriend convinced her to get a tattoo on the back of her arm."

"'Love Leech', do tell! I like the sound of this guy. But first, I need to know about the tattoo, or I won't hear a word you say. But if it is something dumb like two hearts with 'Mom' and 'Dad' written in them, gag me. Sorry, nothing personal, but if that's what it is, then I really don't care."

"Worse than that. It is the Lord Grim. Can you believe that?"

Kara squeals loud enough to turn heads. "WHAT?! That's amazing. Oh, I *have to* see it! Where is

188

she now? Can I tell Kharon? Or Keres? I wish I could still get tattoos!"

Drake sighs and lifts his glass. "This is why I drink." He signals to Tracy. "Another round, please."

Kara scoots closer as Tracy drops off their drinks. "Okay, okay. I'm done. I swear. Tell me about the love leech. What's his name? Want me to check my list? This is why you invited me alone, isn't it?"

Drake takes a slow sip. "His name is Bobby. He is three years younger than Alyssa. He comes from nothing. They met in college. He got in through loans and keeps pushing off repayment by switching majors instead of graduating."

"Oh, honey," Kara says, "do you know the fastest way to get a leech off? Burn it. Too bad you already reaped that arsonist Tiffany. That would've been fun to watch."

"Are you done with your weirdo fantasy?"

"Never."

Drake continues, "He moved in with Alyssa—free housing. Claims he 'lost' his license, so she drives him everywhere or pays for his Uber."

Kara snorts. "Still not leech material. Just a loser."

"Well, he decided they needed pets. Now they have two dogs, two cats, and a boa constrictor. No money to care for any of them. Then he invites his old friend to sleep on the couch because he's 'getting his shit together with his parents.' Another mouth, no help—nobody cleans or cooks. They just order takeout constantly."

"Okay," Kara says, "he's starting to warm up into leech territory."

"And he supervises her social life. Listens to her phone calls. Encourages her—but in a controlling way."

"Oh, that's gross. But you didn't set things up to protect her?"

"There's an executor over the trust—her Aunt Theresa. But she's deadly allergic to animals. The four animals plus Bobby keep her away."

Kara lets out a low whistle. "Ooooh, the man has *skills*. All right, leech confirmed. Every girl gets at least one. Look at me—my boyfriend killed me by accident."

"That's exactly my point. I don't want Bobby killing Alyssa—accidentally or otherwise."

"How would he? You said she's not into anything kinky."

"It's her medications," Drake says, voice tightening. "She takes a lot. For a lot of reasons. And he lays them out for her. He controls which ones she takes.

190

She's fogged half the time. How can she work or meet healthy people like that?"

Kara nods. "Kind of like Britney Spears when she went 5150. Let's hope she doesn't shave her head."

"God, I hope not. And now they're talking engagement. I'm sure she'll be paying for the ring."

Kara's eyes widen. "Ooooh. That's low."

Drake rubs his temples.

"How do you even know all this?" Kara asks suddenly. "OH! Wait. This is why Lady Mercy scolded you for using foresight in the Chamber, isn't it?"

"I don't need to be in the Chamber to use it," Drake mutters.

Kara slaps the table. "WHAT?! You can use foresight on Earth? Not even Kharon could do that! Ugh, I hate you in a fun way. Anyway, watching you stress for the last hour has been absolutely delightful. But I'm not the girl you need. You need the *other* sister."

"Other—what other sister?"

"Lady Love," Kara says, hopping up. "Get Alyssa out from under the spell of love. I gotta run. Keep me updated! Your earthly drama is amazing—I think we could've been friends back then. Ta-ta, love!" She giggles, waves, and skips out the door.

191

Drake rubs his face. Great. Another sister. Mercy, Luck… now Love.

He stares into his glass. What do I even know about love? Other than Donna and Alyssa… what did it mean to me? Does it even exist here? Time doesn't. Why should love?

He lifts his glass for a final sip. "Love is a bitch."

The instant the last word leaves his mouth, the world tears sideways—and Drake is yanked out of the bar.

He lands in a bizarre, swirling realm of gray light and motion. Little movie-like clips flicker everywhere—humans saying the word "LOVE" over and over. Whispered. Shouted. Lied. Misused. Abused. Declared. Texted. Weaponized.

"Love. Love. Love."

It becomes deafening. Drake clamps his hands over his ears. "STOP!"

A voice cuts through it sharply. "Bitch? You kiss my sister's ass and I get called a bitch?"

Drake straightens—and sees the back of a woman standing with her hands on her hips.

"Lady Love." He bows. "Forgive my outburst. I meant no insult."

She ignores him for the moment. "Everyone misuses my name. Look at that woman buying a puppy —'She LOVES it.' In three hours she'll be yelling at it for peeing on the rug. Tomorrow it chews her Prada shoes. And she LOVES her sleep but, because of him, she won't get any. She'll return the puppy in two weeks."

Another vision flickers. A couple whispering "I love you" in secret.

"One of *them* is married," Lady Love says. "He tells his wife he LOVES her every morning. Meanwhile his 'mistress' is actually a catfishing man who loves being an asshole."

The next vision: a 700-pound woman telling a dozen donuts she loves them.

"Closest thing to true love I've seen in an hour," Lady Love mutters. "Tell me, when she finally dies— from the obesity, the diabetes she ignores, the heart that's barely hanging on—who gets to reap her?"

Drake winces. "She wouldn't fall under my jurisdiction. But while the soul carries no weight, the morticians who have to handle her body will hate their shift."

"What exactly do you want from me anyway? Love is no good in your realm." Lady Love finally turns so Justice can see her.

193

Drake freezes.

She is beautiful. Scarred. Blind. A band of old wounds crosses her face, but she stands without apology.

"Hello?" Lady Love snaps for his attention. "I asked you a question. I know you can speak. I heard you a moment ago."

When Justice still doesn't respond, Lady Love starts to laugh. "Oh, you didn't know that love is actually blind?" she teases gently.

"I'm sorry," Justice sputters, reddening, even though she cannot see. "I've heard that saying, but I didn't realize it was literal."

"Love is beautiful, but it never comes without consequence. Like death, it leaves its mark. Love always leaves scars."

Drake finds his voice. "I need help with my daughter. She's alive. She thinks she's in love with this guy named Bobby. She's convinced herself. But I know he'll hurt her. I want your help to break that bond before he does real damage."

Lady Love exhales, the weight of centuries in the sound.

"You're correct—Love is her problem. She has not healed from losing you and her mother. She feels guilty for not being able to save either of you. She is empty, and emptiness is frightening. You filled yours with work and whiskey. She filled hers with caregiving—trying to give Bobby what she couldn't give her parents."

Drake's chest tightens.

"That isn't love," Love continues. "It's grief wearing a pretty mask. And you see Bobby as a leech because you see only your fears. But he is the one who cared for her when you closed yourself off in your grief. And he's the one who stayed when you died. Their bond formed in trauma, yes—but it is real."

Drake frowns. "But—will he change? Will he stop draining her?"

"He will grow," Lady Love says simply. "She will return to accounting. She'll get her CPA. She will work for the FBI in logistics crime. Her work will uncover several major rings. Her faith will return. So will his. Their relationship will strengthen, not break. And Bobby himself will become someone worthwhile."

Drake stares at her.

"And you," Lady Love adds, "weren't exactly adored by your mother-in-law for the first *twenty years* of marriage. Bobby gets the same grace. Come back after twenty years and tell me how their love turned out."

Drake swallows hard. "How do you know all that? Do you have foresight?"

"No," she says with a small smile. "Something stronger. The power of Love. It makes humans do the craziest things. Ask Adam and Eve."

She steps closer. "Leave them alone. Let them be idiots in love. Remember—ignorance is bliss. Let them be blissfully ignorant in love."

Then her expression sharpens.

"Now go do your job. Stop trying to be Dad."

And the realm collapses back into darkness—leaving Justice alone again, chastened, humbled, and—reluctantly—hopeful.

Chapter 25: Who's to Blame?

Does a person's life story begin with the first breath taken, or with the last breath released? So many questions. So many answers.

Who truly gets to tell a person's story? Are we the authors of our own lives, or can our story only ever be told by someone else?

Who knows a person better—a parent or a spouse? And who leaves the deeper imprint—the one who raises you, or the one who walks beside you?

Humans build entire fields of study around these questions. Nature versus nurture. DNA versus environment. Year after year, they design elaborate experiments, desperate for proof that one side matters more than the other. They write papers, argue at conferences, and update textbooks.

Have they actually found an answer?

"Interesting," Lord Grim says, standing behind Justice, looking over his shoulder. Justice sits with a journal open in front of him, pen moving across the page. "I do not recall any of my former Reapers writing down their thoughts about the living."

Justice closes the journal slowly, unsure whether he is being scolded or merely observed.

Lord Grim continues, "I am assigning you to look at Jason Karl, the only child of Norman and Ellen Karl. In the near future, he will alter the balance of life in his state, and ripple outward across the nation."

He fixes Justice with a steady gaze.

"I am not condemning him yet," Lord Grim adds. "But something must change. You will work with the Reaper of Exoneration this time. The two of you will observe and plan together, and decide what to do. My hope is that the outcome will serve all parties well."

Lord Grim vanishes. Justice looks up and notices Exoneration seated a few chairs down, as if he has always been there.

"What do you know about Jason?" Justice asks.

"Very little that is encouraging," Exoneration replies, adjusting his posture and turning toward Justice. "But as Lord Grim said, there is hope. I will share their story, and then we can go observe Jason and his father."

Exoneration folds his hands and begins.

"As Ellen's cancer weakens her," Exoneration says, "Jason takes matters into his own hands. He decides to graduate high school early and becomes her full-time caregiver. In his mind, if his father chooses to be a slave to the 'money game,' then Jason will choose to

198

spend that money on something that matters—every remaining moment with his mother."

He continues, voice even.

"Ellen begs him to stay in school, to stay a kid a little longer. But she is losing two battles at once—her cancer, and her wish to protect her son from growing up too fast. She loses both. She gives in, and welcomes the love and constant presence Jason offers, knowing time is running out."

"When Jason tells Norman what he's decided, Norman simply agrees. No argument. No protest. No discussion. Just a nod, and the conversation ends."

Exoneration's gaze flickers, remembering.

"Ellen fights bravely, but death still comes. The two Karl men do their duty: a small celebration of life, a simple burial. They stand together to accept condolences from family and friends, but they never speak of their grief to each other. Ellen's passing leaves a crater in their home. Norman and Jason walk around it carefully, rather than look into it."

He spreads his hands slightly.

"They move through the house like ships passing at night. Norman cannot express his emotions. He calls anything too vulnerable 'sad talk' and shuts it down. Months pass with barely a word between them. Then one morning Norman announces he is heading back out on the road, back to his long-haul truck routes. He says he will be gone a few days."

"Jason, now eighteen, with a high school diploma and nothing else, decides it is time to start his own life. The only path that makes sense to him leads to the trucking company where his father works. At the very least, he thinks, maybe he will see his dad more often. Maybe he will finally understand him."

"After stacks of paperwork and a handful of perfunctory questions, Jason is hired as a dock worker. Slowly, both Karl men find their own ways to begin again. Time moves on."

Exoneration finishes and looks to Justice.

Justice nods. "That's a lot for one family."

Exoneration inclines his head. "It is. Let us see how they are doing now."

The chamber fades, and the two Reapers stand unseen in the Karl home.

"Hello?" Jason mumbles, rolling over. His alarm clock glows 5:30 a.m.

"HAPPY BIRTHDAY, SON!" Norman's voice blasts through the phone.

"Really, Dad?" Jason groans. "It's five-thirty."

"I guess I'm just excited," Norman replies. "The big one-nine this year!"

"Yeah. Nineteen," Jason says, flopping onto his back and closing his eyes, trying to pry one open enough to function.

"Don't you want to know why I'm excited?"

"Sure, Dad. What's up?"

"Your birthday present is in the gun safe!" Norman says proudly. "I got my hands on a brand-new Ruger AR-556 rifle, fitted with a five-times scope. What do you think about that?"

Jason blinks a few times. "Sounds like a powerful rifle."

"Yes, it is. And I'll be home this weekend. I was thinking we could go to the Northern Sun Gun & Range Club. What do you say?"

"Sure, Dad. That sounds great."

Norman can't tell if his son is excited or half asleep, but decides to quit while he's ahead. "Okay, well, you probably have big plans today, so I'll let you go. See you this weekend."

The call cuts off. Jason watches the screen for a second.

"Bye, Dad. Love you," he says softly to the empty room.

Midafternoon, Jason clocks in at work. Mitch, the foreman, greets him.

"Hey, kid—happy birthday!"

"Thanks," Jason replies.

"I was wondering..." Mitch leans against the counter. "How'd you like the gift of more money? We've got a truck rolling in late tonight. I could use some help unloading and restocking. What do you say?"

"Sure. Sounds good. Want me to clock out at my normal time and back in later, or just stay on?"

"Up to you, kid. That late truck will roll in around eleven."

Jason nods and heads out to the docks.

Once he's gone, Carmen, the office secretary, looks up from her screen. "So, you're not going to tell him it's his old man pulling that load tonight?"

"Damn straight I'm not," Mitch snorts. "Gonna have a little fun with the kid."

Carmen arches a brow. "If I remember correctly, didn't Norman kick your ass right out there on those docks the last time you wanted to 'have a little fun' with him?"

Mitch winces. "Yeah, that happened. Maybe I should change my ways. Or maybe I should treat him like my own kid."

"Is that really better?" Carmen says, flashing him a million-dollar smile.

"You're funny, Carmen. I'm a nice guy," he insists. "I'm giving Norman a few days off to spend with Jason. And I think it's time to bring Jason into the inner circle."

"That's actually a good idea," Carmen says. "He could use people who care about him."

"Right. And the club could use some young blood." Mitch gives her a wink and heads out to the docks.

Night falls quickly. Jason pushes through his overtime shift, muscles sore, mind wandering. At eleven, the deep rumble of an eighteen-wheeler announces its arrival.

Jason checks his watch, hears the brakes hiss, and moves into position with the rest of the dock crew. As the rig backs in, he catches the painted name along the sleeper: Center Mass Shooter.

He grins. That dirty dog Mitch.

He throws a glance down the line at his coworkers. "This is my dad backing in," he calls.

Thumbs go up. Jason heads for the passenger side. As soon as Norman parks, Jason jumps onto the step and swings himself into the cab.

"SURPRISE!" Jason shouts, landing in the passenger seat.

"My boy!" Norman laughs. "I thought I'd be the one surprising you. Oh—careful, you're sitting on your mom's Bible."

Jason shifts, cheeks flushing, and lifts the worn book carefully from under him. He presses a quick kiss to the cover and whispers, "Sorry, Mom." Then, more loudly, "Sorry, Dad. I didn't see it there. I've been wondering where it went."

"Your mother told me to keep it with me always and read it every night before I turn in," Norman says, voice softening. "I've kept that promise."

"That's great, Dad." Jason turns the Bible over in his hands, thumb tracing the edges. In a quiet voice, he

204

adds, "I wish I had something like this to bring her back to me."

Norman's jaw tightens. "Enough of the sad talk," he says briskly. "We've got work to do and I'm starving. Once we unload this rig, we'll grab a bite on the way home."

"Sounds good."

Jason jumps back down and heads to the docks while Norman goes into the driver's office to finish paperwork.

The next morning, as promised, father and son head to the Northern Sun Gun & Range Club. Jason walks proudly behind his father, carrying his new rifle case and ammo bag.

As they enter, several members call out, "Center Mass!"

Jason's chest warms. He knows exactly what that nickname means. His father holds the club record for the most rounds inside a three-inch circle from a thousand yards.

They approach the counter. Brent, the club owner, greets them. "Hey, Norman. Been a while."

"Yeah, been busy. Picking up more routes," Norman replies.

"Will you be shooting today?" Brent asks.

"Nope. Today's about teaching my son, Jason, how to shoot. Can we get a long-rifle lane?"

"Anything for the club's champion," Brent says. "Lane one is all yours." He nods toward Jason. "Enjoy your day, kid. You've got the best teacher."

Norman and Jason nod and head down the corridor.

Walking behind his father, Jason asks, "Do you think I'll get to take a 300-yard shot today?"

"No," Norman says. "Today is about technique and mental discipline. A hundred yards is where you start. Every extra twenty-five yards you move out, you must recalculate—wind, terrain, ammo type, bullet drop."

"Okay. You're the boss," Jason says.

At lane one, Norman sets the rifle case down and begins.

"First rule," he says, "and most important: never point your rifle at anything you are not willing to shoot and ultimately kill: target, animal, or man. Once you point it, you must be prepared to take responsibility. The last two on that list can kill you back."

"Got it," Jason says.

"No, you don't," Norman corrects him. "Not yet. Today, your first job is to listen. These lessons will take time to understand. Today is not about firing as many rounds as you can. Today is about quieting your mind and learning your rifle."

He glances at Jason to make sure he has his attention.

"I'm going to give you the sniper's preparation checklist," Norman continues. "We'll go over it again and again. For now, just listen. This is your homework. These steps need to become automatic—like breathing."

He holds up a finger.

"One: Environmental assessment. You must estimate distance to the target, wind direction and speed, and any difference in elevation between you and the target. Temperature matters too. It affects bullet speed and, in turn, your accuracy."

"Two: Target assessment. You identify the target clearly and pay attention to what surrounds it. You study how the target moves or might move. You anticipate how it could react."

"Three: Mental preparation and visualization. You rehearse the shot in your mind—trajectory, impact point. You see it before you take it."

"Four: Physical preparation. Stance and posture. Stability and balance. You must know your rifle so well that every movement is smooth and consistent. You control your breathing. You relax your muscles. You clear your mind of extra thoughts and focus only on the shot."

"Five: Execution. You engage the target with a calm, controlled trigger pull. And you follow through— keep your eye on the target, maintain your position, and observe the impact."

When Norman finishes, Jason exhales. "You're right. I'm going to need practice."

"With practice," Norman says, "all of this becomes second nature. You'll be amazed—you can time your shot between heartbeats."

"Seriously?"

"Seriously. But you need to get some reps in." Norman gestures to the mat. "Get into position, like I showed you. Pick up the rifle, readjust your body. Good. Now walk yourself through the steps."

Jason starts to repeat them, then stalls. "Dad, I can't remember."

"It's okay. Breathe," Norman says. "I'll give you the steps on paper at home. I have them written down. For now, just remember this: aim small, miss small. One shot, one kill."

"Got it."

"Start small," Norman says. "Go ahead and take the shot. I'll call adjustments."

Jason settles prone, rifle in hand, cheek against the stock, eye to the scope. He whispers to himself: aim small, miss small.

Pop.

"Three inches high, six inches left," Norman calls. "Adjust and shoot."

Jason corrects, repeats: aim small, miss small.

Pop.

"One inch high, three inches left. Adjust and shoot."

Pop.

"Height is good. Over-corrected. Two inches to the right now. Adjust and shoot."

Jason grits his teeth. Sweat beads on his forehead.

Pop.

"Shit! God damn it!" Jason snarls.

"Watch it," Norman snaps. "Look at me. 'You shall not take the name of the Lord your God in vain.' Deuteronomy 5:11."

"Yes, sir," Jason says quickly. "Sorry, Dad. It won't happen again. That was impressive, though—the verse. Mom would be proud."

A flash of lightning cracks across the sky, turning the lane white for an instant. Both men look up.

"Well," Norman says, "that's it for today. You don't mess around when you see lightning. Police your brass, grab the targets. We're heading in."

"But Dad, I was really hoping to get the rifle fully sighted in."

"I already did that," Norman says. "You're the one who needs adjusting. Hand me the rifle."

Jason passes it over. From a standing position, Norman fires three quick shots downrange.

Pop. Pop. Pop.

As he lowers the rifle, someone from farther down the line calls, "Show-off!"

"Who's that?" Jason asks.

Norman tries not to roll his eyes, but Jason catches the flicker. "That's Franklin," Norman says quietly. "He likes to be called Frank. He's Brent's kid brother."

"Collect the brass, then go get the targets," Norman adds.

Jason jogs downrange. The paper target flaps gently in the breeze. He stops and stares. All three of Norman's shots sit in a tight group, center mass.

He pulls the target down and hurries back. As he nears, he hears their voices.

"Come on, Norman," Frank says. "It would help the club and the movement to have the best shooter in the state at our rallies. That new wannabe Governor is running on a platform of complete gun reform. Your son would have to turn that new gift back in."

Norman shakes his head. "I'm heading back on the road. I won't be able to attend. But I'll sign whatever paperwork you need so I can keep my guns."

"How about your son?" Frank presses.

"He's old enough to make his own decisions," Norman replies. "Just not today. I want a little more time with him before I roll out."

Frank notices Jason's approach and lifts a hand. "Okay then. You two take care. We'll be seeing you around, Jason."

211

Jason looks from Frank to his father. "What was that about?"

"Just Franklin being Franklin," Norman says. "He's not only Brent's brother—he's the local NRA president. He's stirring people up against that new governor candidate. One of her big talking points is gun control. Good enough guy, just... intense. If she wins, actually passing anything is a whole different story."

"Interesting," Jason says. "I haven't really heard much about it."

"Here's some fatherly advice," Norman says as they walk toward the exit. "Always educate yourself. Don't believe everything you hear—especially when people are shouting."

Justice and Exoneration watch the Karl men from the edges of the range, then slip back to the in-between.

At Janings Pub, they find their usual corner booth occupied, so they take two stools at the bar.

"Welcome back," Tracy says. "The usual?"

"Yes, please," they answer together.

Tracy sets two shots of Johnnie Walker Blue in front of them. They clink glasses and drink.

"In comes the slithering serpent into the garden of Eden," Justice murmurs, "and all of its temptations."

Exoneration studies the empty shot glass in front of him. "I think I understand our assignment now," he says. "We need to get Norman's attention. Without him, there may be no future for either of them."

"I agree," Justice says. "Are you thinking we reveal ourselves to Norman?"

"Yes," Exoneration replies. "My sense of him is that he will do the right thing when faced with the truth. He will have to choose, like Abraham."

One week remains before the public governor debate. The town thrums with energy. Political signs sprout from lawns like weeds. News vans line the streets. Reporters practice their stand-ups in every available patch of shade.

Gun control dominates the headlines. Everyone in town has an opinion.

Jason keeps his head down but listens carefully to conversations around him at the docks, on the bus, in line at the grocery store. He tries, several times, to talk to his dad about the upcoming debate. Norman keeps cutting him off.

"There's no reason to get involved in all this right now," Norman says each time.

Norman goes back on the road. Jason spends his evenings alone in the big farmhouse, the silence thick and restless. On nights like this he wishes he had something of his mother's to hold onto, the way his dad has her Bible.

A knock on the front door breaks his thoughts.

Jason mutes the TV and walks to the entry. Through the small window beside the door, he sees Carmen and Frank.

He opens the door. "Carmen, Frank. What are you guys doing on this side of town?"

Carmen holds up a covered dish. "We were in the neighborhood," she says with a bright smile. "And knowing your dad is on a long haul, we thought you might enjoy some homemade lasagna."

Jason blinks, caught off guard.

Frank laughs. "So, are you going to invite us in or what? Carmen's lasagna is best hot. We brought everything for a proper family meal."

Jason shakes his head like he's waking up from a dream. "Yes. Yeah—please. Come in. It smells great. Kitchen's this way."

They move into the small dining area off the kitchen. Carmen sets the table, dishes out generous portions, and they dig in.

The food is good. The company feels strangely comforting. They swap stories about coworkers at the docks, the characters at the range, the regulars at the club. There's laughter. Then, slowly, the conversation shifts.

Frank leans back, cradling his glass of iced tea. "We've been impressed," he says. "Your shooting has come a long way. You're loyal to the club. You show up. You put in the time."

Jason shrugs, a little embarrassed. "I just like the range."

"It's more than that," Frank says. "You're helping defend something bigger than yourself. There are people in the capital who would love to come knock on all our doors and take everything. You're standing with us against that. You should know we appreciate it."

He tips his head, voice lowering. "We've also been thinking there might be a role for you to play in the greater good."

Carmen stands and begins gathering plates, moving to the sink to give them privacy while she hums softly and washes dishes.

Jason looks between them. "A role?"

Frank smiles. "Nothing complicated. Just… stay sharp. Keep training. Keep your eyes open as the debate gets closer. There are times when words are cheap and actions matter."

By the time the meal and conversation wind down, the air feels heavier. Carmen dries her hands and returns to the table, wiping a last crumb from the surface.

"Frank, Carmen," Jason says, voice thick, "I really appreciate you coming all the way out here. It was… nice. I haven't had a family dinner in a long time."

"That's because this is family," Carmen says gently.

"That's right," Frank adds. "We look after each other, and we know you'll do the same. Now, get some rest. Get more range time in. That new governor candidate will be doing open public appearances soon. The club won't be meeting anymore—we don't need extra eyes on us. So stay alert. If anything happens, remember where your family is."

"I understand," Jason says. "Thanks for looking out for me. I'll look out for you too."

He walks them to the door and watches them go.

Justice and Exoneration leave the farmhouse and again find themselves at Janings Pub. Their usual booth is still occupied, so they return to the stools.

Tracy sets two more Johnnie Walker Blues in front of them before they even speak.

"On the house," he says. "You both look like you've seen better days."

Justice offers a faint smile. They clink glasses and drink.

"In comes the slithering serpent," Justice repeats quietly, "and all of its temptations."

Exoneration stares into his glass. "We need to move quickly," he says. "I think I see the path now. We must reach Norman before his son crosses a point of no return."

Justice nods, jaw tight. "Then let's go."

The governor debate draws near. The little town is almost unrecognizable—news trucks, campaign buses, extra police. Lawn signs bloom: some for the hard-line incumbent, some for the gun-control challenger.

Jason walks through town like a ghost, pulling on his work clothes, clocking in, clocking out, eyes and ears open. The more he listens, the more certain he becomes that something big is coming.

Norman stays on the road. Whenever Jason tries to bring up the debate, the Governor, or the club, Norman closes the door with, "No reason to get involved in all this right now."

Three days before the debate, there is another knock at the Karl front door.

Jason opens it to a man in a tailored suit holding out an ID.

"Good evening," the man says. "I'm Agent Dwayne Summers, United States Secret Service. I'm looking for Norman Karl. Is he home?"

"Nope," Jason replies shortly.

"Do you know where I might find him?"

"Somewhere in the Northwestern states, probably," Jason says.

Agent Summers smiles faintly. "I see. Maybe if I explain why I'm here, you'll be more helpful. I'm assuming you're his son—Jason?"

Jason opens his mouth, but Summers lifts a hand to forestall him.

218

"Your father is widely respected in this state as the best long-range shooter," Summers continues. "I'm part of the advance security team for the upcoming governor debate."

Jason's eyes narrow. "So, you think my dad is some kind of threat?"

"Not at all," Summers says smoothly. "I'm here to ask for his support and advice. Your father was a fine soldier. He understands defensive strategies better than most."

"Well, if you know that much, then you probably also know he's on the road more than he's at home," Jason says. "Try his company. They know his routes better than I do."

Summers reaches into his pocket and pulls out a card. "Fair enough. If you talk to him, tell him his service and skills are known and respected. That's all."

Jason takes the card and closes the door as soon as Summers steps away.

Three days later, Norman finally pulls his rig into the driveway. The house is dark. No Jason.

It unsettles him, but he tells himself Jason is at the range, or with friends, or maybe just out clearing his head. Norman showers and heads to the kitchen, rummaging in the fridge. As he shifts a carton of leftovers, a business card taped to the door catches his eye.

Agent Dwayne Summers – U.S. Secret Service

Norman frowns, pulls it free, and tucks it into his pocket. He finishes making his meal and tries not to obsess, but Jason's empty room and the silence of the house gnaw at him.

Over the next few days, they keep missing one another. By the time Norman has to leave again, he still hasn't seen his son. He shoulders his bag, heads out to the rig, and turns the radio on.

A news anchor announces, "The governor candidate debate will take place in two days..."

Norman sighs with relief. He will be on the road, far away from what he calls "this freak show."

Feeling unsteady, he pulls out his phone and calls Jason. No answer. He leaves a voicemail instead.

"Hey, kiddo. Sorry we didn't see much of each other. I just want you to know I love you. Be safe."

Hours later, after a long stretch of highway, Norman pulls into a small roadside diner. He needs coffee and a bathroom, in that order.

He uses the restroom, then settles into a booth with a view of his rig. The waitress drops off a steaming cup of coffee and takes his order.

Norman takes a grateful sip and reaches for his wife's Bible, opening it in front of him.

"That's a good book," a voice says.

Norman looks up. Two men sit across from him—he did not see them arrive.

"It is *the* Good Book," Norman answers cautiously. "You read it often?"

"Not for some time now," the first man says.

"That's too bad," Norman replies. "It's an excellent guide. It's nice to sit with other believers."

The second man nods. "We're glad you are a believer," he says. "Because what we're about to tell you may be difficult to accept. It is about Jason."

Norman's posture stiffens. "I'm listening," he says. "But tread carefully."

"As Jason's father," the first man—Justice—says, "you may be the only one who can change his course."

"What's he going to do," Norman demands, "that makes two strangers come all the way out here to tell me?"

"The exact details are not important," Exoneration says. "What matters is that his actions will change his life, yours, and the lives of everyone in your town."

"Who are you two?" Norman asks, eyes narrowing. "And when is he supposed to do this?"

"When is not fixed," Justice replies. "The path is still malleable."

"We work for a higher power," Exoneration adds, "who allows us to take part in determining his outcome. I am Exoneration. He is Justice. We are Reapers."

"Justice and Ex—what?" Norman shakes his head.

Justice glances at Exoneration. "Our time is up," he says quietly. "You will not see us again, Norman. But understand this: if you do not heed what we've told you, Jason will be visited by one of us—and judgment will follow."

Norman stares at them with the same unwavering focus he uses for a thousand-yard shot, looking for any flinch that might tell him this is a joke. Neither man blinks.

They stand.

"Goodbye, Norman," Exoneration says. "Keep your faith."

"Thank you," Norman replies. "And by the way, your watch has stopped."

Justice laughs, looks at his wrist, and says, "Like I said earlier—it has been that way for a long time."

They walk out just as the waitress brings Norman's dinner.

He looks up at her, then at the plate. "Actually," he says, "can I get that to go?"

Later, back in his truck, Norman calls Jason again. No answer. He sends a text instead:

Trust is earned, not in a moment, but over time. The people giving you advice may be speaking from their own scars.

He pulls onto the highway, but his hands are slick on the wheel. He calls the office and finally gets Carmen.

"Hello, this is Carmen. How may I help you? ... Hello?"

Norman sees a billboard flash past: *Train up a child in the way he should go; even when he is old, he will not depart from it. – Proverbs 22:6*

"Sorry, Carmen," he says after a long pause. "It's me. Norman."

"Oh! Norman. Is everything alright?"

"Yes. I think so," he lies. "Have you seen Jason?"

"Yes," she says. "He's been at work every day. It's been crazy around town with the debate tomorrow. I think we'll be closed—everyone will want to be there. I'm sure he will be. I'll let him know you called."

"That's kind of you," Norman says. "One more question. Does he seem... okay to you?"

"Well, you know how it is," Carmen replies. "Office staff and dock workers don't cross paths much. But he seems fine. Why? Is something wrong?"

"I'm coming home," Norman says.

"Norman, you know you can't do that," she says gently. "If you don't finish this delivery, you'll lose your job."

"You might be right," he answers. "See you tomorrow."

He ends the call and turns the rig around.

As he drives, he prays. For guidance. For protection. For clarity.

After twelve hours on the road, he finally pulls into his own driveway—two hours before the debate. He parks his rig on the road and hurries inside.

The house is empty, as expected. He moves through the rooms at a near trot. In Jason's room, he finds a flyer from the gun club about the debate. A sloppy bullseye is drawn over the liberal Democrat candidate's face. Beside it lies Jason's phone, its SIM card removed.

Norman swallows hard. He drops the flyer and rushes to the gun safe, praying with every step.

He opens it and stares. Jason's new rifle is gone.

Norman's jaw hardens. He lifts out his own McMillan TAC-338 sniper rifle and a ten-times scope.

He loads up and leaves.

The roads into town are choked with political signs and cars. Norman drives past the local sheriff's checkpoint. The deputies wave him through; they know him by name.

But as he approaches the second checkpoint—a wall of state troopers in unfamiliar uniforms—he veers off, taking side roads and country lanes only locals remember.

He reaches a hillside roughly two thousand yards from the debate's outdoor stage. From here, he can see the church tower, the crowd, the banners, the press. Far enough away that no one is looking back in this direction.

He sets up, drops prone, and settles behind his scope. He sweeps the crowd. He spots the security teams, coworkers, familiar faces from the docks and the range.

No Jason.

On stage, Reverend Earl Staples welcomes the candidates and invites them to take their seats. The moderator waits in the wings. The crowd buzzes.

Norman breathes slowly, scans again. This time he finds Jason—high in the church tower, rifle braced, eye pressed to the scope.

Norman can see his lips moving.

Aim small, miss small. Aim small, miss small.

Time freezes. The sound of the crowd fades. In the silence, Norman hears one clear sentence:

Take the shot, or I will take your son.

He closes his eyes and fires a quick, desperate prayer heavenward. Then he opens them, lines up his sights—not on the candidate, but on his own boy—and squeezes the trigger.

The round crosses two thousand yards and slams into Jason's scope, shattering the glass as the anti-gun candidate steps up to the podium. The shattered lens blows back into Jason's face.

Jason jerks away, blind in one eye, blood running down his cheek. His finger never touches his trigger.

He stumbles from the tower and is rushed to the hospital.

Days later, Norman sits in a hospital room with his wife's Bible open on his lap. Jason lies in the bed, one eye heavily bandaged, pale and groggy from surgery.

Norman reads quietly, lips moving. A soft tap on the door makes him look up.

A smartly dressed man stands in the doorway.

"Your office said I'd find you here," the man says. "Norman Karl?"

Norman rises, closes the Bible, and steps into the hallway, pulling the door gently shut behind him. "What can I do for you?"

"I'm Agent Summers," the man says. "Secret Service. I thought you might want to know about an incident at the governor debate."

"What kind of incident?" Norman asks, voice level.

"There was a single rifle shot heard by the crowd," Summers says. "But no one was injured at the event.

When the team searched, they found broken glass and blood in the church tower, but no sign of a gun being fired from there. So the file is closed. Whatever happened must have occurred on private property."

Norman nods slowly. "Thank you for letting me know. As you can see, my son just had surgery. I'd like to get back to him, if you don't mind."

"Of course," Summers says. He hesitates. "Just one question, if you'll indulge me. Best distance shot ever?"

Norman blinks once, twice. "No," he says quietly. "My absolute worst."

Summers studies him, then says, "Spare the rod, spoil the child."

Norman replies automatically, "Proverbs 13:24."

Summers nods. "All will be exonerated," he says, and walks away.

Chapter 26: The Murder of Alyssa Themus

As Lady Love foretold, Alyssa Themus does, in fact, build a life with Bobby.

She finishes her degree and goes on to Purdue, where she earns a master's in accounting and a second B.A. in criminal justice. She sits for the exam and becomes a Certified Public Accountant. From there, the Federal Bureau of Investigation recruits her to the Chicago field office, placing her in logistics and financial analysis—corporate espionage, corruption, and dirty money that snakes back into the federal government.

On a gray Monday morning, Alyssa sits through the standard briefing: ongoing cases, fresh intel, follow-up on matters nearing indictment or trial. When it's done, the department head, Lisa, calls out as people stand to leave.

"Alyssa, hang back a minute. I've been told you have visitors," Lisa says. "I'd like to sit in. They look like 'agency men.'"

"Any idea why they're here?" Alyssa asks.

"No," Lisa says, "but it won't hurt to hear what they have to say."

They walk together to Conference Room Two. Inside, two men sit waiting—matching black suits, crisp white shirts, shoes polished to a mirror shine. The only difference between them is their ties: one red, one black.

The women don't feel underdressed in their bureau-regulation black slacks, black shoes, and colored blouses, but there is no missing that these men have dressed to impress.

When Lisa and Alyssa enter, both men rise.

"Hello," the one in the red tie says. "I'm Agent Ryan, and this is my partner, Agent Connor." They hold out their credentials.

Lisa and Alyssa glance down at the badges, then up again. Alyssa can't help herself.

"So," she asks, "is Ryan your first name or your last name? Or is it both?"

The two men exchange a look. Agent Ryan's jaw tightens.

"We didn't come here to talk about names," he says.

"Okay, then, Agents," Lisa replies smoothly. "What brings you down to FBI Logistics?"

"We're following up on the fine work Agent Themus did on the Grilkar Corporation," Ryan says, "and their inside informant, Helena Clark."

"That case has been closed for four months," Alyssa says, her tone turning flat and official. "We're waiting on the congressional hearings on September second. Ms. Clark is in protective custody, and we're under court order not to discuss the case."

"We're aware of that," Connor says.

"Then why are you even involved?" Alyssa asks. "Your agency isn't allowed to operate inside the United States. Legally."

"We're aware of our limitations," Ryan answers, "and of what is considered legal for both agencies."

Lisa cuts in. "Okay, I'm going to end this meeting here. Submit whatever request you have through proper channels so everything is documented and tracked. You can see yourselves out."

The women stand. The men do the same. Lisa and Alyssa wait until they leave the conference room, then watch them disappear down the hall.

Only when the door closes does Alyssa exhale. "Why is the CIA circling back to a case our department closed four months ago?" she asks. "What are they fishing for, and who are they answering to?"

Lisa looks her dead in the eye. "Alyssa, listen to me. Be very careful. I know you don't want protection. I know you don't carry a firearm even though your badge allows it. But be careful. I don't want you to get shot 'by accident' in a Starbucks, like other people who… disappear."

"Really?" Alyssa asks. "You think I'm in trouble?"

"In trouble, no," Lisa says. "In danger, very much so. Those two are CIA, but they don't answer to the same government and justice system we do. Go back through everything in your transcripts. Every name you listed. Where the money came from. And more importantly, where it went."

A week later, Alyssa sits in Lisa's office, a folder open on her lap, eyes bright with anger.

"You're not going to believe this," she says. "They're still moving money offshore. Shell companies, stacked inside shell companies. And some of those shells connect to current congressional seats."

Before she can continue, Lisa raises a hand. "Stop."

Alyssa blinks. "But—"

"This is why I told you about those two CIA agents," Lisa says. "I called in a chip with a friend at NSA the minute they left. They're technically part of a branch spun off from the South America division. Peru, to be precise—which just happens to be where a large chunk of your money trail ran through. Your work cut their operating costs by fifty percent."

"Okay," Alyssa says slowly. "So why am I in danger, again? For doing my job?"

"Because a bullet costs thirteen cents," Lisa says quietly. "What happens if you start naming names could cost someone who doesn't care millions of dollars. And those people might be the very ones asking you questions—or the ones writing the laws we try to enforce."

Alyssa stares at her. "What are you not saying?"

"I'm not sure our prosecuting team will move ahead with the congressional hearings in September," Lisa replies. "They may decide this case is too expensive."

"Expensive?" Alyssa demands. "What does money have to do with this?"

"Not expensive in dollars," Lisa says. "Expensive in lives. I mean I am worried about your life. I am asking you to back off and let it go. The top people at Grilkar are dead and gone. Let them stay that way, before you join them."

"That's just it," Alyssa says. "They're not gone. Yes, Richard McDonald and Lewis Drey are dead from their own stupidity, but their replacements are already waiting in the wings. New faces, same crimes. That's what I want to fight."

"Alyssa, you're not hearing me."

"Are you going to fire me if I don't stop?"

"No," Lisa says. "But I want you to think about this: this is one small thing. There are plenty of other fish —and whales—out there who need you to catch them."

On June sixteenth, the Washington Post headline reads:

FBI WITHDRAWING PROSECUTION AGAINST CONGRESSMAN PLATTNOR

The first paragraph tightens Alyssa's fists around the paper:

Congressman McCarthy Plattnor is named as one of the main recipients of "kickback" monies from the now financially spiraling Grilkar Corporation. Grilkar was cited for widespread mishandling and falsifying stock records.

Disgusted, Alyssa marches straight into Lisa's office.

"What is this?" she demands, holding up the newspaper. "Why didn't you tell me? I've found more proof of foul play, and I think it's still going on."

"Because we are logistics analysts," Lisa says evenly. "Not field agents. We win our fights on paper. This case moved up and out—we're not part of it anymore."

"Did you see the additional corrupt funding that's surfacing?" Alyssa asks. "This isn't over. It's just beginning. I want to be ready for the hearings."

"Alyssa, listen and listen well," Lisa says. "Your part is over. Drop it now. Go take a walk, clear your head. Get some coffee. I'll have a new assignment for you this afternoon."

Taking the advice, Alyssa walks across the street to the coffee shop. She waits at the counter for her iced coffee, scrolling her phone with one thumb.

"Excuse me," a voice says. "FBI Logistics Analyst Alyssa Themus, right?"

She turns. It's Agent Ryan, red tie and all. Connor stands beside him.

"It's good to see you again," Ryan says. "Do you come here often?"

Alyssa stares at him and lets her irritation surface. "I don't know," she says. "You tell me if I come here often, CIA Agents First-or-Last-Name. Or should I call you Tweedle-Dee and Tweedle-Dumb? Do you come here often?"

A smirk curls Ryan's mouth. "We both love coffee," he says. "Just like everyone else in here. Don't we, Tweedle-Dee?"

He and Alyssa both look at Connor, who smiles and nods.

Ryan continues. "We're just glad to see the additional names you added to your reports won't actually see the light of day. So maybe we can get coffee somewhere else, and never bother you again."

"You know there are other ways to get justice against these criminals," Alyssa says.

"Yes," Ryan answers calmly. "We know how justice can be handed down."

"Is that a threat?"

"Enjoy your iced coffee, Alyssa," he says. "Before it gets watered down."

Back at the office, Alyssa takes her new case file from Lisa, sits at her desk, and starts taking notes. Numbers. Names. Patterns. Hours pass.

Her phone buzzes on the desk. She frowns when she sees the caller ID.

Bobby. He knows better than to call her during work. Which is exactly why she answers.

"Hey, Bobby," she says. "Everything okay?"

He is talking, but nothing makes sense. It's a stream of noise and breath.

"Slow down," she says.

He only speaks faster. She thinks he might be crying.

"BOBBY!" she shouts.

Silence.

She pulls the phone back, checks the screen. The call is still live. She brings it back to her ear. "Bobby, what happened? Are you alright?"

A sniff. A shuddering breath. Then his voice, shaky.

"I just got home," he says, "and all our pets have been killed."

Alyssa blinks once. Twice. Three times. "How?"

"I don't know," Bobby says. "The carbon monoxide detector isn't going off. I don't smell gas."

"Do you think anyone is still in the house?" Alyssa asks. "Are all the pets accounted for? Even Kitty?"

"No one's here. I checked everything before I called you." He swallows. "And yeah. All the pets. I used the word 'killed,' not 'dead,' for a reason."

Alyssa's stomach drops. "Bobby, this doesn't make sense. I don't understand."

"Both dogs are in the kitchen," he says. "Dead, but not shot. Kitty... she's gone. She's been fed to Boa. I checked the whole house. No one. Nothing broken. I'm going to call the cops now. This is wrong, Alyssa. This is sick."

"Don't touch anything else," she says. "Wait outside until the cops arrive. I'm on my way."

She grabs her bag and bolts. As she passes Lisa's office, she leans in.

"I'm headed home," she says. "Bobby needs me. The cops are on their way."

Lisa looks up, already grabbing her keys. "What happened? Never mind. Go. I'll call you—no. I'm coming with you."

238

They arrive to find Bobby sitting on the front porch, white as a ghost. Alyssa runs to him and folds him into a hug. Lisa walks to the cluster of uniforms emerging from the house, identifies herself, and listens grimly as they brief her.

Alyssa and Bobby sit on the porch, fingers laced together, clinging to each other. When Lisa approaches, her face is set.

"Okay," Lisa says. "From their assessment, there's no sign of forced entry. Nothing stolen, no damage. Just the two dead dogs and the cat, which your snake is... eating."

Alyssa's jaw tightens. Bobby just looks hollow.

"I checked the dogs myself," Lisa continues. "I think they were sprayed in the nose with some kind of chemical. Probably killed them. I'm having our team take the bodies—we'll run necropsies, find out what the chemical was."

Bobby stares at her like she's grown a second head. "They can do autopsies on dogs?" he asks. "We also have cameras. Security sensors. Did the cops check those?"

Ignoring the first question, Lisa says, "All your systems were disabled. Professionally. Nothing was recorded. Nothing tripped."

Alyssa bites down on the inside of her cheek. "This might be nothing," she says, "but Ryan and Connor 'ran into' me at the coffee shop today. We didn't talk case details, but the vibe was bad. Lisa... do you think this could be them?"

"A warning?" Lisa says. "Yes. A shot across the bow."

"You mean a shut-up shot," Alyssa says.

"Either way, it's a warning," Lisa says. "You're officially off the case. I'm ordering you to turn over all your files. Hopefully, that gets back to whoever is watching you, and they back off. Which means you back off."

"Okay," Alyssa says finally. "I get it. I'm done. I'll turn everything over to you tomorrow."

"Take the night," Lisa says softly. "Meet our coroner team when they pick up your dogs. See me tomorrow. I'm so sorry this happened. I'm glad you're both okay."

The next morning, Alyssa gets to work and finds Lisa and Lisa's boss already waiting by her desk.

"Good morning, Alyssa," Lisa says. "I thought it best to get this taken care of first thing. I'd like you to meet Division Head Elijah Silverson. He's joining us from the Illinois division."

Alyssa sets down her coffee and bag, nods to Silverson, and notices the stack of file boxes beside her desk.

Silverson walks over, lays a hand on one of the lids. "Is this everything?"

"Yes, sir," she says. "It is."

"Agent Themus," he says, "you do excellent, thorough work. I'm glad we didn't lose you."

"Thank you, sir."

"As Lisa has already told you, it's best to let this one go and dive into a new case," he says. "Dismissed."

On August twentieth, the Wall Street Journal, New York Times, Washington Post, and USA Today all run similar headlines:

FEDERAL BUREAU OF INVESTIGATION LINKED LEAK

The articles suggest a cover-up: additional payoffs, new connections to Congress, hints that prosecutors are choosing not to pursue anyone.

On September second, under pressure from the White House, Congress and the Senate open an investigation into the now-suspended Congressman Plattnor.

In a safe house somewhere far from the cameras, Agent Ryan folds one of the newspapers and drops it on a table.

"Well," he says to Connor, "looks like we're heading back to Chicago."

Connor gives him a sly smile. "Good," he says. "I liked the coffee. Any special requests? Car accident? Suicide? Random shooting?"

"Speed," Ryan says. "That's the only requirement. It has to be done before our dear FBI logistics analyst Alyssa Themus can be subpoenaed and dropped into protective custody."

"Is she the unnamed leak?" Connor asks.

"Doesn't matter," Ryan says, standing. "We need to move."

For months, Justice resists the urge to use his foresight on his daughter. When Lady Mercy and Lady Love scolded him, he listened—mostly. He focuses on his work as the Reaper of Justice, searching the world for names that belong on his list.

Then he sees one.

The name itself isn't familiar. But the feeling it triggers is. A dread that belongs, specifically, to Alyssa Themus.

He reaches, just once, toward her thread in the tapestry. The vision slams into him: a sanctioned hit on his daughter's life.

Fear crashes over him.

When the vision releases him, Justice does the only thing he can think to do. He calls a meeting at Janings Pub—with Murder.

He sits in his usual booth, hands wrapped around an untouched glass, when Kharon slides into the seat across from him.

"No fancy whiskey waiting for me?" Kharon asks, arching a brow.

"No," Justice says. "All business this time."

"Too bad," Kharon says. "The Johnnie Walker Blue is the only thing I like about you. What do you want?"

"I've seen it," Justice says. "An unnecessary murder. My daughter, Alyssa. I want it stopped."

Kharon leans back, expression flattening. "Remember," he says, "I'm Murder, not Justice. I don't have foresight anymore. My job is to clean up the mess, not prevent it. And since it's my job, not yours, I'd strongly advise you to stay out of it. We've already had this interference argument once. Grim sided with me."

Justice clenches his jaw. He says nothing.

The bar lights dim for a moment. When they come back up, Kharon is gone.

The week passes. Nothing happens. Alyssa goes to work, comes home, tries to live a normal life with Bobby. The new puppy tumbles around the house, clumsy and joyful, filling some of the void left by the dead pets.

On Saturday, September thirteenth, Alyssa stands in the kitchen chopping peppers for dinner. Bobby wrestles the puppy into a harness by the back door.

"Okay," he calls, "I'm headed out. Back in about an hour. Love you!"

"Love you!" she calls back.

She hears the front door shut and lock. She goes back to slicing peppers, letting the rhythm soothe her.

A moment later, she hears the back door open again.

"What did you forget?" she calls over her shoulder.

"I forgot to clean up my mess before I left the first time," a man's voice replies.

Alyssa freezes.

Agent Ryan steps into the kitchen.

She turns slowly, knife still in hand. "I'm not alone," she says. "My husband's upstairs."

Ryan tuts softly as he moves further into the room. "Tsk, tsk, Agent. You shouldn't tell lies. We watched him leave. He'll be gone about an hour. That's plenty of time." He tilts his head. "Do you know how many homeowners actually arm their security system while they're inside?"

Another figure moves in behind him. Agent Connor steps into view.

"No need to answer the alarm question," Connor says. "The answer's zero. And because I do think you care about this answer—the dogs didn't suffer. Heart attacks. Quick deaths. Well. Almost quick."

He reaches into his jacket and slowly draws out a small metal canister with a mask attachment—an aerosol weapon. He starts toward her.

The moment he moves, Alyssa throws her knife.

It leaves her hand in a clean, practiced motion and buries itself in Connor's right eye. He drops to the floor without a sound.

Ryan stares at his partner's body. "Well, that's a shock," he says. "Your record says you barely qualified with your pistol."

"Records don't cover everything," Alyssa says, breathing hard but steady. "My dad taught me during Covid lockdown. We both got good with knives. My record's accurate—I'm not great with a gun. But my knife skills are deadly. Walk out the way you came, or die like your partner."

"That won't be happening," Ryan says calmly. "This should've been quick. Now we need to call a cleaner. So I might as well just shoot you."

Alyssa spins back toward the counter to grab another knife as Ryan pulls his pistol. She pivots, arm raised, knife ready—

The muzzle flash blooms before she can release the throw.

Everything goes dark.

246

Bobby arrives at the Mount Sinai emergency room white-faced, the puppy tucked in his arms. He stands just inside the sliding doors, head snapping left and right, until a voice cuts through the noise.

"Bobby, over here," Lisa calls, lifting a hand.

He hurries over and drops into the seat next to her. "What's going on?" he asks. Now that he looks, he sees them—FBI jackets scattered through the waiting room. "Did something happen to Alyssa? Where is she? Why are all these agents here?"

"Bobby," Lisa says gently, "there was an incident at your house this morning. We don't have all the answers yet. Alyssa is in surgery right now. We don't have an update yet, but I'll tell you what we know as it comes."

"I don't understand," Bobby says. "Everything was fine when I left. When can I see her?"

"Once she's out of surgery and in a private room," Lisa says. "Then you'll be allowed in. There will be twenty-four-hour security on her until we understand what happened. I'm sorry you're going through this. I'm here with you. Is there anyone we should call?"

"Maybe Mrs. Asboth," Bobby says, looking down at the puppy in his arms. "Our neighbor. I need someone to take care of Angel while I'm here with Alyssa."

"Okay," Lisa says. "We'll have an agent take Angel over. She already knows something happened—she's the one who called 911 when she heard the gunshot. Most of her family are Chicago cops."

"Did she call you?" Bobby asks.

"No," Lisa says. "After the... dog incident, I flagged your home. Any 911 call from your address or immediate area is supposed to ping me."

Illinois Division Head Elijah Silverson walks over. "I'm sorry to intrude," he says. "Lisa, I need a word. Bobby, I'm sorry for what you're going through."

Lisa stands and goes with him to a quiet corner. She listens, shoulders tensing visibly, then nods. "Thank you, sir," she says.

When she returns, Bobby is staring at the surgery board, waiting for any change next to Alyssa's case number.

"Bobby," Lisa says carefully, "I'm sorry, but you won't be able to go home for a few days. The house is now an active crime scene. You can stay here under protection, but if this drags on, we'll move you to a secure hotel under twenty-four-hour detail until the investigation is complete."

"Security?" Bobby asks, eyes still fixed on the screen. "Investigation? Why?"

"Two men were found dead in your kitchen," Lisa says. "Where Alyssa was attacked. One had a paring knife in his eye. The other…" She hesitates. "We're not sure what happened to him. One of our agents said it looked like a two-hundred-ten-pound man had every bone removed and been left on the floor like a human rug."

Bobby finally turns to look at her. "Do you know who they were?"

"I can't say more yet," Lisa answers. "Both had weapons. The one with the knife in his eye was carrying an aerosol delivery system. The other had a gun. If you need anything from the house, we can send someone to pick it up. For now, please understand: this situation is dangerous until we know all the players. That's why we'll be protecting both of you. We will do everything we can to get justice."

She does not say what both of them already fear—that sometimes, justice comes too late.

Chapter 27: Fight to the Death

Drake sits in Janing's Pub with a bottle of Johnnie Walker Blue tipped to his lips, drinking straight from it the way he used to when he wanted his worries to vanish. The liquid doesn't offer the usual escape tonight. Not even close.

The door slams open. Kharon stomps inside, hood low, faceless fury radiating off him like heat. He marches straight to Drake's table.

"What is wrong with you?" he snarls. "You had no business being there and messing up my reaping. I do plenty of work for those government-hired assassins. And you didn't even save her! She's still in the ICU!

"I get you served 'justice' on that one agent, and I took the one your daughter killed, but what you did was sloppy. You let your anger act out. Ripping all the bones out of someone and leaving the body there to be found is just dark. Even for you."

Drake grinds out, "I know. And shut the hell up. That's my daughter."

"Was your daughter," Kharon spits. "She hasn't been yours since you died. And she'll belong to me soon enough."

Drake's expression hardens. "I don't care what you or anyone else says. I'll stop you."

"Your job is Justice," Kharon growls. "Right now there is no justice. There's just us. So tell me—what exactly are you going to do?"

Drake swallows a final mouthful of whiskey, then spits it out—igniting it as it leaves him. A burst of flame hits Kharon's chest. He staggers backward, patting out the fire.

"Just so you're aware," Kharon says, brushing off glowing embers, "nothing humans use can hurt either of us on Earth's realm. But when we use it on each other? It's as lethal as anything they do."

He moves in a blur.

Kharon kicks the table square into Drake's chest, sending him crashing backward over his chair. Before Drake can recover, Kharon is on him—fists raining down, cracking across Drake's jaw, ribs, temple.

Tracy rushes over with a sawed-off shotgun, shouting, "Knock it off! BOTH OF YOU—"

Kharon turns, backhands him effortlessly. Tracy flies across the bar, slams against the front door, and collapses, dropping the shotgun as he falls.

That tiny distraction is all Drake needs.

He snatches a heavy beer mug and smashes it across Kharon's head. Kharon reels. Drake shoves him off, climbs on top of him, and holds him down long enough to shout:

"Everyone OUT! And take TRACY!"

The bar patrons scramble, dragging Tracy with them.

Kharon breaks free, grabs Drake's hair, and slams their foreheads together. Drake staggers backward, dazed. They rise at the same time, throwing wild, punishing blows. Drake catches Kharon with a solid left hook, then sweeps his legs, sending him crashing to the floor again.

Drake lunges for Tracy's shotgun. He opens it— both barrels loaded. He snaps it shut and aims it as Kharon climbs to his feet.

Kharon smirks. "Go ahead. Hit me with your best sh—"

The blast cuts him off. Drake fires one barrel. The shot tears through Kharon's hooded coat, slamming him into the floorboards. Smoke curls from the ruined fabric.

Kharon coughs. Laughs. "WOW. That was unreal."

He rolls onto his knees and slowly stands, bracing himself against the wall.

Drake stares. "How? Why aren't you dead?"

"Dead?" Kharon grins. "We're both dead, Drake. Have been for a long time. This fight isn't about dying. It's about staying in existence at all."

Kharon steps closer, voice darkening.

"When I became the Reaper of Murder, I started taking a fragment from every murderer whose victim I reaped. Thousands and thousands of little soul-pieces. Murderers lose parts of themselves; I take those parts. They strengthen me. Rebuild me. That's why I always look different, sound different." His voice deepens, distorts. "I cannot be destroyed."

He charges.

Kharon slams into Drake, tackling him around the waist. They crash into the bar. The shotgun jerks in both their hands. It fires—obliterating the liquor display behind them. Bottles explode. Glass and alcohol rain down as sparks from broken lights ignite a roaring inferno.

Flames climb rapidly. Heat blasts the room.

The two Reapers fight through it—hands locked around each other's throats, choking, slamming, grappling, punching. The explosion that follows blows out the front window and hurls them both into the street —

—and in the blink of an eye, they're no longer in the earthly realm.

They crash to the floor of the Great Chamber, each landing on opposite sides of the massive "V" table.

War stands there, stunned. He wasn't sure why he felt summoned—until now.

Drake and Kharon rise. They don't care where they are. They only care about finishing this.

Overhead, their birds—Devon and Mayhem— shrieking, tear into each other in a vicious aerial battle. War watches them, entranced, as the two Reapers resume their brutal clash below.

Blows are exchanged without pause. They grab broken chair pieces—fragments of Disease's seat—and strike with them like clubs.

Elder and Accident appear. Elder screams for them to stop like a desperate mother yelling at two sons hell-bent on killing each other. When they ignore her, she hides behind War, horrified and sobbing, before fleeing entirely.

Accident, by contrast, runs circles around the fight, cheering wildly. "KILL HIM! BOTH OF YOU! YES —YES—MORE!" Each near-fatal strike makes her squeal with glee.

War steps forward to shield Elder, setting his massive war maul on the table—

And Murder lunges. He grabs the maul and swings with all his force.

Justice barely dodges. The maul smashes into the right wing of the "V" table, exploding it into rubble. Drake is thrown backward into the wall from the force of it.

Murder pauses. Smirks. "Look at that. Finally paid you back for what you did—cracking our side of the table with Grim's scythe. Now I'll break *you* the same way."

From the shadows, Seppuku appears. Silent as ever, he draws his katana, then tosses it to Drake.

"Defend yourself," he whispers.

Drake catches it.

The two Reapers clash—steel against supernatural flesh. Every strike lands harder than the last. Murder swings downward with the maul. Drake blocks, sidesteps—and slices.

Murder's left hand falls clean from his wrist.

It hits the stone with a wet thud. Silence follows.

Murder stares at the stump, then at Drake. Slowly, Murder drags the maul with one hand.

"Murder… it's over," Drake warns. "Surrender so we can end this."

"Surrender?" Murder laughs, deranged. "Never. I've been faceless for ages and still function. You think missing a hand matters?" He lifts the stump—and before their eyes, the hand regenerates. Fully formed. Perfect.

"I am the most dangerous Reaper. Even God warned you in the Ten Commandments—'Thou shall not murder.' I am NEVER ending."

He flexes the new fingers.

Drake realizes the sword isn't enough.

He hurls the katana toward Murder's chest. Murder bats it aside with inhuman speed. The blade crashes into Seppuku's chair.

Drake charges before Murder can recover. He grabs him under the arms, lifts him off the ground—

—and drives him backward onto the blade of Lord Grim's scythe.

Murder is impaled clean through. His body hangs there, motionless.

War retrieves his maul. Seppuku retrieves his sword. The chamber falls silent as all the Reapers watch, waiting to see if Murder regenerates.

A raven's caw cracks through the silence.

Devon dives from the rafters, Mayhem clutched in his talons. He slams the rival crow onto the broken table, snapping its neck and wings. Devon rips out Mayhem's eyes one by one, then carries the corpse up and through the open left doorway—straight into Hell.

Every Reaper present understands.

Kharon—Reaper of Murder—is no more.

Lord Grim appears on his throne. Murder's body dissolves from the blade of the scythe, fading without ash, without smoke, without a trace.

The role of Murder now stands empty.

Chapter 28: What is Your Final Decision

The Great Chamber stays silent until Lord Grim fully materializes upon his throne. When he plants the butt of his massive scythe against the stone floor, the echo rolls through the hall like thunder. In an instant, all the Reapers—and Lady Mercy—appear in their seats around the great "V" table. Every gaze settles on Lord Grim as he gives a small nod, signaling that they should be seated.

He speaks.

"Since the time of Genesis 4:8, when Cain rose against Abel and murdered him, there has always been a Reaper of Murder. The souls of those taken by violence cannot remain long among the living. Their reaper must come for them swiftly—it is unnatural for them to linger."

He scans the table, voice deepening.

"The one who holds that title has changed over the ages. When Erikl abandoned the mantle of Justice and took on the role of Murder—becoming Kharon—I allowed it. He was too far gone to serve any other purpose. And so the seat of Justice remained empty, as justice so often is."

His grip tightens on the scythe.

"Today, for all of you to witness, I enact a choice I have made once before."

His gaze lands on Drake.

"Drake Themus, Reaper of Justice. I will ask this question only once—just as I did when I first offered you your mantle. I now ask you to become the new Reaper of Murder. If you accept, the change begins instantly. You already know how to reap. Your abilities will be reduced to those of your peers."

He pauses.

"If you refuse, you will proceed to Judgment for your earthly life. Nothing you have done as a Reaper will be counted against you. You will no longer interact with us—or with Earth—ever again."

The chamber holds its breath.

"What is your final decision?"

Drake answers, voice flat and resigned. "I will serve as the Reaper of Murder."

"So be it," Lord Grim declares. "Let all here bear witness. A new Reaper of Murder rises this day. The seat of Justice stands vacant once more."

In the next instant, Drake—now Murder—is transported to the ICU surgical suite where his daughter Alyssa lies dying, machines keeping her organs alive only long enough for the donor network. Her body looks small, pale, still.

He whispers a prayer. "Lord God… have mercy."

A soft voice responds behind him.

"Did you mean Lady Mercy?" She steps into view, serene and sorrowful. "Yes, Drake. I may still interact with you. But it is too late for mercy for those who have already left the living realm. Only the next Reaper of Justice may help the departing, as you once did."

She touches his arm gently. "When she changes, have Devon carry her to the Great Chamber. It may be the only moment you two have to speak before she moves on."

"Thank you, my Lady," Drake says.

He turns to Alyssa. When he touches her cheek, the color drains from her body. Above them, Devon shifts —black feathers tightening, form sharpening—no longer a raven but a crow, bound now to Drake in his role as Murder. With measured care, the bird lifts Alyssa's soul and carries it into the Great Chamber.

Alyssa walks alone toward the massive "V" table, disoriented. Quick flashes hit her—light, a gun muzzle, the soundless bloom of impact.

"Over here, Alyssa. It's okay."

She turns. Her father stands there.

"Dad? How did you... how are you here? You died. I cremated you. I put you with Mom like you wanted. Where are we? Am I dead? What is—"

"Yes. An offer. Yes again. Thank you. The Great Chamber. And yes."

She blinks. "What?"

"Those are your five questions answered in order —quickly—so your mind can settle. You've got a thousand more, I know."

She exhales shakily. "I feel like crying, but I can't. Dad... why can't I?"

Drake motions her closer. "Let me tell you my story. From the moment I died, to becoming the Reaper of Justice, to everything I learned in between. Mercy. Judgment. Foresight. And the long, tragic history of those who carried the role before me."

He tells her everything—his training, his struggles, about the other Reapers, about the chamber, the battles, his new role as Murder, and why he has been the one standing over her since the moment she died.

Alyssa listens, stunned, then finally says, "Okay. I... I think I understand."

Another voice fills the chamber.

Lord Grim has appeared again.

"You claim to understand how and why you stand here," he says. "Then you will understand the single question I will now ask you."

Alyssa and Drake stand together as Grim addresses her directly.

"Alyssa Themus, I offer you the mantle of Reaper of Justice. If you refuse, you may proceed to your eternal judgment beyond those doors."

Alyssa steps forward. She lets go of her father's hand. She faces Lord Grim.

"I accept. I will take the role."

Lord Grim nods. "Excellent. From this moment, you are Justice. Murder, return to your reaping. I will introduce Justice to Lady Mercy."

—

Drake and Alyssa return to the earthly realm, choosing Janing's Pub as their first meeting place. The windows are boarded, but the sign on the door reads: *OPEN DURING RECONSTRUCTION.*

Inside, Tracy is directing workers.

"Tracy!" Drake calls. "I'm glad you're alive after… everything. And sorry about the damage."

Tracy grins. "Man, they told me *you* dragged me out. I owe you big. And get this—I didn't even know the previous owner left a multi-million-dollar property policy attached to the place! I'm rebuilding better than ever. You'll always have a drink here."

"You still serving Johnnie Walker Blue?" Drake asks.

"Damn right."

Drake nods at Alyssa. "Two rounds. One for me, and one for my daughter."

Alyssa wrinkles her nose. "Ugh, whiskey? Nice to meet you, Tracy. I'll start with this, but I'll figure out my own drink later."

They take their glasses to a more private corner.

"This is the earthly meeting place I told you about," Drake says. "Janing's."

"It's nice," Alyssa says. "And Tracy seems great. But he doesn't know what we are."

"No—and no one with a soul ever should. Now… have you thought about your first assignment as Justice? I lost my foresight when I became Murder. I can't see what's ahead anymore."

263

Alyssa studies him.

Then she says, with absolute conviction:

"Congress."

Chapter 29: Forgive Me Mother

Drake decides he needs a little R&R and heads to Janing's Pub. Before he goes, he calls Seppuku to join him. The two reapers sit together, sharing rounds of Johnnie Walker Blue as Seppuku tells quiet stories of ancient Japan—battles, honor, discipline, things older than memory.

Elder appears beside Seppuku without warning.

"Pardon the interruption, Drake," she says softly, urgency beneath the calm. "I need you to come with me. We must go now."

Drake immediately rises. "Of course. Whatever you need."

"Thank you," Elder replies, already turning. "I will explain more very soon. Please—come."

The two Reapers disappear.

When they reappear, Drake feels a jolt of déjà vu. The hallway. The faint smell of antiseptic. The muted light. He knows this place—not as a Reaper, but as a son.

"Why are we here?" he asks, a tremor in his voice.

Elder looks at him gently. "I think you already know."

Drake turns toward the door at his right. Slowly, he reads the nameplate.

Carol Themus.

His breath catches. "Why... why are we outside my mother's room?"

"I think it is best if we go in," Elder says softly, passing through the door.

Drake follows.

Inside, his mother lies sleeping peacefully, her hair silver against the pillow. An open Bible rests on her lap—her hand still near the page, as though she drifted off mid-verse. The soft rise and fall of her breath is faint, fragile.

Elder steps closer to Drake and whispers, "Do you recognize her?"

Drake's voice is flint-thin. "Yes."

Inside, emotion floods him—regret, love, memories he has avoided ever since becoming a Reaper. He realizes how deliberately he has refrained from looking in on her, even with foresight.

Elder senses all of it. She leans closer again. "Speak to her. She will still hear your earthly voice. There is time. Do not squander it."

Drake steadies himself. He moves to her bedside, kneels, and speaks softly.

"Forgive me, Mother... for anything I ever did that hurt you. I love you."

He bends and kisses her forehead.

Elder asks gently, "How shall we appear to her?"

Drake draws in a breath. "She always told me angels with great white wings would carry her to heaven."

Elder smiles faintly. "That sounds lovely. So be it."

Together they stand as Carol Themus takes her final breath. Her body fades to colorless stillness, and her soul rises—escorted by the shimmering image of an angel with wide, white wings. She is lifted toward the light beyond.

Drake watches, peace settling across his features.

"How long until someone finds her?" he asks quietly.

"In about six hours," Elder answers. "Her breakfast group will notice she's missing. They will alert the staff, and a welfare check will follow."

Drake nods. "May I sit with her until then?"

"Yes," Elder says. "And may your memories be good ones."

Everybody dies.
What matters is not death itself—
but who comes to reap your soul.

These are their stories.

Lord Grim.
The Ladies of Eternity.
And the Reapers who serve them.

ACKNOWLEDGMENTS

Co-Writer & Editor: Erin MacKellar
Art & Design: Alyssa Dorrin, Morgan Janing

Special thanks to the friends and family whose ideas, experiences, and even personal tragedies helped shape this story— and to those who graciously allowed me to let fictional versions of you die on the page: Devon Lauffer, Bella Hoyle, Robert Prado (twice), Priscilla Trejo, Jessica Armedariz, Tracy Motley, and Carol Lauffer.

Most of all, to my forever-loving (and very much alive) wife Dana—thank you for your constant support.

And finally, thanks to God, through His Son Jesus, for the promise that no matter which Reaper comes, He will be waiting on the other side of the judgment doors.
John 3:16

About the Author

Kurtis Lauffer was born in Northwestern Pennsylvania and served with honor in the U.S. Army's 3rd Infantry Regiment at Arlington National Cemetery.

After earning his Mortuary Science degree from Gupton-Jones College in Atlanta, he built a 30-year career as a licensed mortician in Arizona, where he continues to serve the community. He has also held leadership roles, including President of the Arizona Funeral, Cemetery, and Cremation Association.

A devoted Christian, husband, father, and avid poker player, Kurtis brings a lifetime of experience at the intersection of service, loss, and humanity to his writing—always hoping his stories resonate with readers long after the final page.

Kurtis is currently working on his second novel, a sequel to Reaping: The New Justice.

www.ingramcontent.com/pod-product-compliance
Lightning Source LLC
Chambersburg PA
CBHW052039240626
47153CB00006B/2150